Donovan's Revolution

Michael Loyd Gray

Copyright © 2024 by Michael Loyd Gray
Donovan's Revolution
Oprelle Publications, LLC

All rights reserved. No part of this publication may be reproduced, distributed, or transmitted in any form by any means, including photocopying, recording, or other electronic methods without the prior written permission of the author, except in the case of brief quotations embodied in reviews and certain other noncommercial uses permitted by copyright law.

For information address:
Oprelle Publications,
236 Twin Hills Rd.
Grindstone, PA 15442.

FIRST EDITION

ISBN: 979-8-9899015-3-1

Donovan's Revolution

Dedication

My late mother, Dorothy Gray, would have enjoyed this book, and so I dedicate it to her memory and the wonderful support she gave me. I always say I got my writing talent from her.

Thanks, too, to my dear old friend in Germany, Anthony Squiers, who is a brother and a great sounding board about writing but also about life and staying the course.

I also want to thank my longtime personal editor, Carol Burbank, at Storyweaving. Her insightful reactions to my novels enable me to make wise decisions about revisions.

And I want to recognize writer and editor Katie Gantt, a great friend from when I taught in Aiken, South Carolina.

Finally, where would I be day to day without the constant companionship and mischief of my amazing cats, Suzie Lucifer and Yoda Lucifer. They watch over me when I write.

Chapter One
Haiti, 1985

The bus from Port-au-Prince lurched along muddy roads. Black smoke belched from the exhaust, coloring thick humidity. Passengers hung heads out windows and pretended there was a breeze. Donovan Prentiss got out twice to help push the bus from deep muck, and when they stopped in a village of dirty, sagging shacks, he asked its name and was told it had none. Listless children were a dull black and lean, and one boy's ribs were clearly visible, but he smiled gamely. Donovan gave him half of an Almond Joy. Far off, Donovan saw a majestic peak of barren slopes.

"That is Pic La Selle," said Gilles Daladier, a Haitian that Donovan judged to be about forty. "It is the tallest mountain in Haiti."

Gilles worked for the Diocese of Port-de-Paix, which sent him to fetch Donovan to Les Cayes, a coastal village southwest of Port-au-Prince. Donovan's mandate was to be optimistic, cheerful, and "do what he could." It was vague enough to offer some latitude, he figured.

"Just how high *is* that hill?" Donovan said.

"Nearly three thousand meters," Gilles said. "That is almost nine thousand feet."

"I reckon that makes it a mountain after all."

"By any definition," Gilles said flatly. "It is no hill."

"It would be much cooler up there, that's for sure," Donovan said.

"Maybe you would like to climb it—to be cooler, of course. That would be more fun than what you will have in Les Cayes."

"I'm not too worried about having fun," Donovan said firmly.

"Well, on Pic la Selle, you would surely be much closer to God."

"You think so, Gilles?"

"Closer than these miserable wretches down here."

Donovan could see that Gilles's faith had sprung a leak or two. And did anyone still use the word wretches? That seemed straight out of Dickens, or perhaps Austen. But Gilles's English was otherwise quite good.

"If only there was time for mountain climbing," Donovan said. "But Rome didn't mention that. So, I'll pass."

"You would not want to deviate from Rome," Gilles said flatly. "Or in general, to be a deviant of any kind."

"To be sure," Donovan said emphatically and nodding.

"But that happens here anyway."

Donovan forced a smile and changed the subject. It was too hot to speak of deviants.

"Still, it's quite beautiful here, Gilles."

"Yes, it is," Gilles said. "Once you get past the poverty and starving children and peasant revolts and government indifference, of course."

"Of course. But other than that—"

"Yes, other than that, quite beautiful."

"A paradise, really," Donovan said.

Gilles stared at him.

"It must seem so to you."

"To *my* eyes, anyway."

"Your eyesight will improve," Gilles said. "You have just arrived."

"And I've yet to really see what's here."

"You see jungle out a window and a mountain far away," Gilles said. "And then a little boy smiles at you for a candy bar. So, tell me, who did you double cross in Rome to get sent here?"

Donovan chuckled lightly.

"I was told it's an *opportunity*."

"Oh, yes—to be sure. It is *that*."

"And after all, the Pope himself was here just two years ago," Donovan said.

"Yes," Gilles said. "Indeed, His Holiness was. But he wisely went home. You are here to stay. You sense the difference, correct?"

Donovan nodded and smiled.

"I grasp it, yes. But like I said, at least it's an opportunity."

"The road of good intentions is paved with them," Gilles said.

"Is that the road we're on?"

"If it helps to think so, then yes."

After a while, Donovan said, "Gilles—your name means servant of Jesus, doesn't it?"

Gilles smirked. "Yes. But promise me you will never call me that."

"Don't you serve Jesus?"

"I get paid to take you to Les Cayes in one piece. I serve

the ones paying me. Jesus does not pay me."

"No faith?"

"Look around—where is Jesus in all this?"

Donovan pretended to gaze in earnest out windows on both sides of the bus.

"Well, he sent *me*, didn't he?"

Gilles looked at him neutrally for a moment and then smiled and slapped Donovan's knee.

"Why did you not say so? Now I know all will be well. Haiti will be corrected. This is good indeed."

"But perhaps not in one day."

"Of course not," Gilles said. "You will need more time. Two days, perhaps?"

"Better make it three."

"Of course," Gilles said. "That makes more sense. After all, you are not God."

"And I wouldn't claim to be."

"A wise choice."

Donovan smirked at Gilles's ability to be smarmy and insolent at the same time. A rare gift, he supposed.

"By the way, Gilles... what happened to the priest who used to be in Les Cayes?"

"You were not told?"

"No."

"He took to drinking every day," Gilles said. "The rum is excellent. I can recommend it. I even prescribe it – daily."

"He became sick?"

"No," Gilles said, laughing softly. "He became naked. He walked the beaches naked. Well, you can imagine the reaction. And he was not a man with a body for nakedness, I can tell you."

"I see."

"Do you?"

"Of course. The man obviously had reached his limit."

"No," Gilles said. "There were no longer any limits at all to him."

"How so?"

"It is said he molested several women. And a boy, too. See? No limits. He had not reached a limit—there were none at all."

"An extreme case, Gilles."

"Perhaps. If you choose to think so. Do you plan to drink yourself past the limits, Donovan, and run naked on the beaches?"

"I think not. And I brought a swimsuit."

Chapter Two

The first thing Donovan learned about Les Cayes was that it certainly *looked* like a postcard from paradise: coral reefs, coconut palms, white sandy beaches on a turquoise sea, and mountains behind the town covered with lush green vegetation.

But the second thing he learned was that it was *not* paradise because food was in short supply and President Duvalier's promises of reform were empty rhetoric. And there really was no church, just a house with a makeshift cross on an outside wall and inside a few tables and chairs on worn wood floors. His quarters were a set of rooms in the back of the house with a separate entrance. There was a bed, a table, and a tiny bathroom.

Donovan had been sent by the Vatican. Well, not by the Pope, of course, who did not know that Donovan even existed, and instead someone much lower along the food chain, a minor functionary who probably had never seen the inside of Vatican City. Someone not even a priest. Donovan had made connections in Rome because he had once studied there to be a priest – quite briefly at that – after graduating from Michigan State, but he abandoned those studies when he couldn't tell himself exactly *why* he should be a priest.

He'd enjoyed exploring the ideology but never could decide what it all added up to, what he might do with the knowledge. In the end, he realized religion interested him *somewhat*, intrigued him as a sort of philosophical puzzle to solve, but it did not consume him, nor stamp a mark of identity on him. And he grew suspicious of the peacock pageantry of Catholicism, the militarized hierarchy that rendered it, to him, simply a gaudier version of the endless empires that stalked the earth.

Donovan worked for Rome as a sort of contractor, a civilian fixer who could be sent to places in need when no priest was available. Hired help. An interim solution. He was an envoy of sorts but had no official title and no formal mandate other than to do what he could until a priest could be sent. To those he tried to help, he was simply known as the man from Rome.

They often believed he really was a priest, and he tried to dissuade them at first but learned it was hopeless to try and advantageous to let them believe it. That's how he managed to do any good at all, although he always wondered if he really did accomplish anything. Maybe comforting people and assuring them things would get better qualified as doing good. But it seemed a tad thin to him. It had become mostly a mediocre paycheck and a place to sleep.

There was little good to be done in Les Cayes. Comforting people quickly seemed pathetic—and dangerous. By the end of his first week, riots broke out in the streets, and people stormed food centers. Some of them were shot by panicky government troops, and Donovan heard bullets pass close above his head like angry bumblebees as he helped two men pull a wounded woman off the street and onto the portico of a building as troops swept by and drove the crowd down the street.

There was a moment he would never forget as he leaned over the woman to try and comfort her while one of the men tore a strip from his t-shirt for a tourniquet to wrap around her leg: her eyes fluttered and she sighed slowly, and as Donovan held her hand, he felt the barrel of a gun touch the back of his head. It was held by a young soldier, just a boy really, his face sweaty and uncertain, and then the boy soldier smiled and walked away. Donovan felt he might lose control of his sphincter. He began to tremble, and to himself, he prayed, too. The boy soldier waved and ran to catch up with the other soldiers.

The woman lived, Jeremy learned later, but other rioters, including children, were killed by soldiers who lost control of themselves. Jeremy saw the bodies lined up just off the street. They had begun to swell in the heat, like pictures of the dead Jeremy had seen in photos of the American Civil War. But the photos from books were not enough to prepare him for the real thing. Flies had already begun to cover them. The stench was like fish rotting under a hot sun.

Donovan didn't want to look at the bodies but felt he must. A real priest would, he reasoned. There were two young children, a boy and a girl. Both had been shot in the head. The girl's jaw had been blown away and brains leaked from the boy's head. Donovan managed to remain composed long enough to step behind a building and throw up. He vaguely wondered how well a real priest would have done.

He thought to go back and say a prayer for the dead and do what he could for the survivors, but soldiers herded people away from the bodies and Donovan lost his nerve and crossed the street and sat stunned in the shade of a portico. Across the street, the young soldiers meandered around the bodies and smoked cigarettes. They kept looking down the street as though they expected more trouble.

An agitated officer showed up after a while and ordered them to load the bodies in a truck. Donovan watched from across the street. He wanted to leave but something made him stay and watch. The soldiers tossed the dead rudely into the truck's bed and laughed each time one landed and made an ugly sound, the arms and legs of the dead flopping awkwardly as if the dead were simply drunk and not dead. Donovan winced each time one landed and bounced.

After the truck drove away, Gilles showed up.

"Baby Doc will blame the church, of course," Gilles said.

"The church is just trying to help," Donovan said, his voice lacking conviction.

"That's how wars start. A church tries to help."

"Do *you* have any suggestions?" Donovan said with some exasperation.

"I do what I'm paid to do and no more."

"Yes, I know, Gilles. Jesus doesn't pay you. You've mentioned that before."

"At least with me, you know where you stand."

Gilles convinced him to go with him to a bar down the street. There Gilles poured rum into a shot glass and slid it across the table to Donovan, whose nerves had still not settled. They were the only ones there except the old man from behind the bar who kept looking out the window at the empty street.

Donovan picked up the glass and stared at it for a moment.

"Baby Doc," he said. "It sounds vaguely obscene."

He downed the shot and put the glass down hard enough that it tipped over, rolled off the table, and shattered.

"Another casualty of the revolution," Gilles said, attempting to smile. The bartender looked over at them a moment and then back out at the street.

"Do you think it's really a revolution?" Donovan said.

Gilles poured himself another drink. The bartender brought another shot glass and then swept up the glass.

"It has been a revolution for some time," Gilles said. "There was also a revolt in Gonaives before you arrived. Before that, protests in many cities. It has always been a revolution, but now it's getting bloody."

"Is Baby Doc really as bad as they say?"

"I imagine he is worse than what they say," Gilles said. "What is said is only a fraction of the truth. I have heard he sells body parts as well as drugs."

"How do you know that?"

"People in Port-au-Prince told me."

"What people?"

"People who would know."

"Government people?"

"Yes," Gilles said. "Baby Doc people."

"But not loyal to Baby Doc?"

"They are paid to work for him," Gilles said. "But very few people around such a man are truly loyal. They are bought. And being bought can expire."

"Then it must be bad, I guess," Donovan said. "What's coming, that is."

"Very bad, Donovan. Evil. He is a degenerate. But he will go. It is only a matter of time. But maybe much time.

That is hard to know."

"He won't just go?"

"No. He must be *made* to go."

Donovan accepted another shot of rum and downed it.

"Well, we can still do some good here," Donovan said.

"Yes—we can help pick up the bodies and then drink our rum. It is really very excellent rum."

"Are you on the side of the rum?"

"I am on *my* side, Donovan."

"Well, the church is on the side of the people, Gilles. I represent the church, if rather loosely. I must comfort these people when I can, as best I can."

"A brave speech," Gilles said. "And how long can you do that?"

"Until it's all over—until Baby Doc gives in. Or is made to go."

"Do you think that will be soon, Donovan? He has money and many soldiers with many guns."

Donovan studied Gilles' face for a moment.

"Where were you when the shooting started?"

"Not on the street, I can tell you that."

"Where?"

"Does it matter?"

Donovan slid his glass over to Gilles to be refilled.

"No, not really."

Chapter Three

Soon after the riots in Les Cayes, Baby Doc Duvalier cut food prices and even fired some of his cabinet, but he also deployed more troops around the country and his reform efforts were revealed as insincere and short-lived and led to even more oppression. Uprisings continued, and in Les Cayes, there was talk of resistance fighters in the hills beyond the town.

The diocese financed a ramshackle hospital with European volunteers and a few Haitian doctors and nurses to house the people wounded in the riots. Donovan visited every day and prayed for those who could not speak and joined in prayer those conscious enough to pray for themselves. He didn't have to be a priest to pray with them, for them.

Government troops would sometimes walk through the hospital carrying AK-47s. They would smile and say hello to Donovan and call him Father, even though he explained he was not a priest, but he knew they were there to be menacing in even a subtle way and to remind people who had the firepower.

One day, soldiers shot a man stealing food from a food

center and they left his crumpled, bloody body in the street and refused to let anyone remove it all day until they felt everyone had had a chance to see it. A group of soldiers sat on a store portico drinking rum to make sure no one moved the body. The heat had begun to blow the body up and flies descended on it in swarms. By nightfall, the soldiers took their rum party down to one of the beaches and gunfire could be heard in town as they drunkenly emptied AK clips into the surf.

A rumor spread that several young women were raped by the soldiers but it remained unconfirmed, though Donovan had learned that it could just as easily be true. Haiti was no paradise, despite the postcard scenery, and he now saw it as something of a hell to be endured. He wondered how long he would be in it and whether he might not even survive it. He resolved to keep going and do his best because he felt like a trapped rat that must keep fighting while looking for an exit.

The next morning, the poor wretch shot in the street – yes, he decided, wretch was a word for Haiti after all – had been carted off and buried and his family came to him later to pray, even though he explained he was not a priest. But he prayed with them and felt quite inadequate as he did, and knew it was all symbolic anyway and the family did seem, finally, to appear soothed a little by his ministrations. Or maybe they were just better than he was at absorbing pain. Their pain was greater than his, but his was palpable.

***

Toward the end of the week, after Les Cayes had been unusually quiet a few days, many of the soldiers boarded trucks carrying their AKs and extra ammo clips and water and grenades, and several carried rocket-propelled grenade launchers. Donovan watched them climb into the trucks, many of them looking quite serious and even a few seemed to be scared, he thought. The trucks roared down a street leaving dust clouds and people came out of buildings and stood on the street and on porticos and watched. A few soldiers were left behind to guard the food centers and he guessed there would be no more visits to intimidate people at the hospital for a while.

The next evening, two young men were brought to the hospital while he was there. Both had been wounded, but not too badly, he would later learn. One had a grenade fragment in a shoulder and the other had a bullet pass cleanly through his leg without hitting bone. One of the Haitian doctors cut the shirt off the man hit in the shoulder, and a nurse unwrapped the bloody field dressing off the other man's leg. Donovan marveled at how stoic the wounded seemed but later was told they had been given morphine on the trip in. They had been helped in by other men in dirty fatigue clothing and Donovan saw that one of them was Gilles; except Gilles was dressed as usual in a white shirt and wrinkled white slacks. He did not seem to be with the men and yet they glanced at him deferentially. A silent leader.

Gilles waved Donovan over.

"Where are the soldiers, Donovan?"

"The ones they left behind, you mean?"

"Yes," Gilles said. "And the others—have they returned?"

"No. No trucks have come back yet. Who are these men?"

"A hunting accident, Donovan. No need to concern

yourself."

"Gilles, I know you believe I'm naïve, but do you think I'm stupid, too?"

Gilles studied his face and then grinned thinly.

"Sorry. That was... unkind of me."

"Who are they?"

"Resistance fighters. Rebels. There was an action this morning."

"Fighting? We didn't hear anything."

"It was on the far slopes, in the jungle. You would not hear anything. It took much of the day to carry them down here."

Donovan looked at the wounded men and had a realization.

"Are there others? Was anyone killed?"

Gilles looked down at the floor a moment and then away, out a window.

"Yes, men were killed. It was quite a fight. The soldiers had RPGs."

"Yes, I saw them when they left."

"The RPGs were a nasty surprise," Gilles said.

He looked momentarily shaken, an emotion Donovan was not used to seeing from Gilles.

"How many of these resistance men were killed, Gilles?"

Gilles continued to look out the window at the street.

"About a dozen."

"And the soldiers?"

Gilles looked back at him and nodded.

"Many of them died, too."

Donovan went to the window and looked at the street. It was quiet.

"Gilles, the soldiers will have wounded. They'll come

here."

"I'm sure they are on the way now, Donovan. But they foolishly used their trucks to see if they could cut off the rebels beyond Bauzan. Some of their wounded will die because of it—but that is *their* problem."

Gilles went to the Haitian doctor and urged him to work quickly. Donovan looked again out the window but saw nothing.

"Gilles—*did* they actually cut off the rebels beyond Bauzan?"

Gilles shrugged his shoulders.

"I do not know. I helped bring these men down here."

"This is very risky. What if some of the soldiers at the food centers come down here?"

"They won't leave their posts until the rest of them return," Gilles said. "And once the doctors do their work, we will move these men somewhere safer."

"You're *with* these men, Gilles?"

Gilles looked over at the two wounded men a moment and then at Donovan. He smiled thinly.

"It is a long story, my friend," Gilles said, patting him on an elbow. "And I could use a drink. How about you?"

* * *

Later that night, Donovan met Gilles at a bar near the beach—the same one they drank in on the day of the first food riot and when Donovan stared down the barrel of an AK-47. The same old man bartender brought them glasses of Rhum Barbancourt. The only other patrons were a group of older men at the far end of the bar. Gilles looked them over several times and, to Donovan, appeared to finally be satisfied they were just old men drinking rum and laughing about something.

Gilles sipped his glass of rum.

"Have I ever told you, Donovan, that the rum here is excellent?"

"On occasion, Gilles. On occasion."

"It is because of the sugarcane juice instead of molasses."

"Good to know, Gilles."

"Even better to drink."

Donovan sipped his rum.

"Those two wounded men—where did you take them, Gilles?"

"Somewhere safe. Outside of town. It is not something you should know."

"Fair enough. How are they?"

"Lucky. They will live."

"That's good. I suppose I should pray for them."

"I suppose you should. Will you pray for the government wounded when they show up, too?"

"They're already here, Gilles. I heard the trucks as I walked down here. But I'll avoid the hospital as long as I can."

"Wise," Gilles said. He got up and walked over to a window and looked out for a moment and then went to the bartender and gave him money. He returned to the table with a bottle of rum.

"It is not safe here. Let's walk down to the beach."

They walked to a place where tall rocks were offering a view all the way back up the beach toward the bar and town. They passed the bottle between them.

"Who are you, Gilles?"

"Just a man, Donovan." He looked up the beach but

there was no one and it was quiet. The sound of the surf dropping on the beach was the only sound.

"But *whose* man, Gilles?"

"Does it matter?"

"Yes, it does—and don't give me that I work for the diocese and Jesus doesn't pay me bullshit."

"Good for you, Donovan. You have teeth after all. Yes, those days are long past, I suspect."

"You're with the rebels?"

"I did not exactly say that."

"But you showed up with them. I have to tell you, Gilles, there were times I had you down as one of Baby Doc's men. Even a spy, perhaps."

"Such little faith in me, Donovan."

"I don't know you."

"Well, I am no Baby Doc man. I lost friends in Port-au-Prince to Baby Doc. Good friends."

"I'm sorry. But it's time to level with me."

"No, first *you* must level. Where do *you* stand with the rebels?"

Donovan pondered it a moment.

"Well, I'm sure not a Baby Doc man. How could I be?"

"You say you help the people," Gilles said. "Well, the people are fighting to make Baby Doc go away. Where do you stand on that?"

For the first time, it was clear enough for him.

"I stand with the people, Gilles."

"And the rebels?"

Donovan turned and looked out over the moonlit Caribbean. It sure didn't look like a place that would be marred by so much violence and death. He turned back to Gilles, who handed him the bottle and he sipped from it.

"The rebels... are inevitable, I suppose," Donovan said.

"You condone them?"

"I'm just a man. Sound familiar?"

"No, you are not just a man. You represent the church here—even if you are not a priest."

"Words spoken for a different age, I think."

"Maybe so. But who *do* you represent, Donovan?"

"Myself, Gilles. I'm working for myself now."

Donovan felt it was true for the first time. He was no longer Rome's man. Maybe he never was. It was just a job. He was still a man with some faith, but he did not think he was an extension of the church in this place. He was just a man trying to do what felt right... and survive.

"Welcome to the world," Gilles said. "We are all working for ourselves in the end."

Donovan stared at Gilles in the dark and could not quite make out his face.

"Do you really work for yourself, Gilles, or someone else?"

"I work for the CIA."

"My God."

"An appropriate enough reply," Gilles said. "Maybe you should pray for me, too. I will not be offended."

Donovan sagged in his chair.

"The CIA—here?"

"Who do you think is behind the resistance? Who do you think provides them arms? Where do you think the morphine we gave those two men today came from?"

Donovan accepted the bottle from Gilles and had a good pull from it.

"What happens next?"

Gilles took the bottle back and sipped.

"The revolution continues. The fighting continues. It cannot be put back in the bottle and placed on a shelf. The genie is out. I cannot tell you more than that."

"I don't *want* to know more than that," Donovan said. "Not tonight, anyway."

Chapter Four

The next day, Donovan went to the hospital expecting trouble from government soldiers, but he discovered there were only three government wounded and the rest of the troops had been loaded back onto their trucks and left town again. As Gilles had predicted, the government commander had allowed most of his wounded to die as he vainly pursued the rebels, who slipped into the jungle beyond Bauzan.

Donovan left the hospital without seeing the wounded and so he was able to avoid praying for them. He said a prayer to himself for the rebels in the hills and walked through Les Cayes until he found Gilles sipping coffee at a café.

"I'm ready to know more," Donovan said.

"Sit down, my friend. Have some coffee."

"It's too hot for coffee."

"It is never too hot for coffee. It is one of the few civilized pleasures around here."

"That and rum, I guess."

"You are learning."

As Donovan sat down, two government soldiers walked

by the café, their AKs slung over their shoulders. They glanced at him, and he turned away and looked into the café as the soldiers passed.

"Do not look paranoid," Gilles said. "They will smell your fear."

"*I* can smell my fear."

Gilles smiled and sipped coffee.

"Just do not be so obvious," he said. "Act as though nothing is the matter. They know you. They accept you are here from the church. It is an excellent cover."

"And they don't know who *you* are."

"I certainly hope not," Gilles said. "That must remain our little secret. I prefer to remain among the living."

A few minutes later the soldiers came back but passed by without even glancing at the café. Donovan watched them disappear down the street.

"A routine patrol," Gilles said. "Nothing more."

"What about the rebels?"

"What about them?"

"What's happening with them?"

Gilles looked at his watch.

"Perhaps right now some are having lunch.'"

"And after lunch?"

"They will scatter into the jungle. They will re-form soon enough."

"Catching their breath, I suppose."

"And working up their courage again, I suspect."

"And then what?"

"I do not know," Gilles said. "I have not talked with them."

"But you're CIA."

Gilles reached over and grabbed Jeremy's wrist firmly

for a moment.

"Do not ever say that in public. Do you understand?"

"Yes, I understand." Donovan jerked his wrist away. The waiter brought him coffee and he sipped a moment and looked down the street again, where the troops had gone, but he didn't see them. "I just thought you would know what happens next. That's all I was saying."

"I advise them, Donovan. And make sure they get what they need. I do not command them."

"Who does?"

"They have someone."

"Who?"

"You do not need to know that."

"What *do* I need to know? It seems I know plenty as it is."

"This is not America, Donovan. Or Rome. It is Haiti. A very dangerous place. There are things you do not want to know. Things that can get you killed."

"I'm in this now, Gilles. I was in it as soon as I saw your men at the hospital."

"They are not *my* men. I just advise them."

"They're your countrymen. This is your country."

"Actually, I was born in France," Gilles said. "Paris. My father was French, my mother Haitian. But I am certainly *fond* of Haiti. Or I would not be here. I would ask out."

"I wish *I* could ask out."

"I do not doubt it," Gilles said with a laugh. "Have you considered it? Just tell the diocese you want to go home. Or you could get drunk on the beach like your predecessor. That, too, is an effective tactic. But, please, if you decide to molest anyone like he did, stick to women. It will make it somewhat easier for me to like you."

"So, we're friends, Gilles?"

Gilles stared a moment and to Donovan, it appeared he was assessing his answer.

"I prefer us as friends, Donovan."

"As opposed to an enemy?"

"I cannot afford you as an enemy—not with what you know."

"I know nothing, then."

"That is good. For your sake as well as mine."

"And for the sake of the revolution."

"Without a doubt. But the revolution goes forward no matter what happens to us. The revolution is bigger than us."

"Then let's make sure nothing happens to us, Gilles."

"I would toast to that if we had some rum."

"I've had enough rum for a while."

"I have *not*," Gilles said.

"Tell me this, Gilles—why did you tell me who you are at all?"

Gilles waved the waiter over to refill his cup. Donovan declined a refill.

"Because now you are working for yourself," Gilles said. "As you mentioned last night. I think you see the success of the rebels freeing you from Haiti. And the church can be an asset in all this. You represent the church."

"So, I'm an asset to be moved around a game board?"

"That is perhaps too… clinical."

"I fantasized you would say it's because you trust me."

"Do not be so serious all the time, Donovan. I will trust you as much as I can trust you."

"Wow—that much."

"Trust is earned," Gilles said.

"How do I earn it?"

"The people trust you and the government troops accept your presence. You can walk in both camps, as it were."

"I'm a spy? An informer."

"Informer is ugly, and spy is perhaps too dramatic—too James Bond."

"I always liked James Bond," Donovan said.

"How about... scout? Very romantic, too. Like in those wonderful American westerns."

Donovan smiled.

"Don't tell me that a half-French, half-Haitian man whose true identity can't be mentioned is also a fan of American cowboy movies."

"The western novels, too, Donovan. I'm especially fond of the work of Louis L'Amour. A hobby."

Donovan laughed.

"My father has a whole slew of those books. My mother says they're trashy and makes him keep them on a shelf in the garage."

"What does your father do?"

"He fixes cars. He can fix anything on wheels."

"An honorable profession."

"And not as complicated as all this," Donovan said. "Help me get out of Haiti, Gilles, and I'll send you the whole L'Amour collection."

"You must want it very badly to steal from your father. Very naughty for our man from Rome."

"Let's not look at it as stealing, Gilles."

"How *should* we look at it?"

"Let's think of it as reallocating assets to a good cause."

"Theft," Gilles said, chuckling. "But I like how you put it. Maybe we recruit you."

Donovan leaned back in his chair and crossed his arms across his chest.

"Now, tell me, Gilles, since I work for you now, what my first assignment is."

Gilles finished his coffee and looked down the street a moment.

"Drop by the food centers," he said. "Many of the soldiers fancy themselves good Catholics, even though they work for Baby Doc."

"And just what do I do at them?"

"Be friendly. Ask them if they need anything. Invite them to confess, for God's sake. One of them might slip up and tell you something we would like to know."

"I can't use the confessional to spy on them, Gilles."

"You do not have to. Just hang around them and see if they will confide in you. They all think you are a priest – not a spy."

"Scout—remember?"

"Of course – scout. More dignified, to be sure."

"Okay, then," Donovan said, standing up. "I'll see what I can do. Where can I find you later?"

"I will find *you*."

Chapter Five

Donovan had not seen Gilles for several days. There was no word about the rebels in the hills beyond the town and the government troops had been quiet, too, preferring to stand guard at food centers or to stay close to their barracks. Donovan did his best to get information from soldiers but didn't think he learned anything significant at all. They were friendly but did not seem to take him seriously. He didn't want to disappoint Gilles, but he felt the soldiers were not likely to tell him much, even though they believed he was a priest.

For a while, Haitians would stop by the little church Donovan lived in and they would pray or ask him to pray for them. Telling them he was not a real priest had no effect and he stopped saying it. Lately, no one had come by, and he grew tired of sitting around so he went down to the beach to watch people and eat red snapper and diri kole ak pwa – rice with red kidney beans. He washed it down with a cold Prestige, a popular Haitian lager, and ordered another one.

There was a Haitian woman in a large floppy yellow hat sitting at a table nearby. She was quite pretty and had long dark hair flowing across her shoulders under the hat and Donovan figured she was in her early thirties. He could not recall seeing her in Les Cayes before. She smiled at him when they made eye contact.

"You are the American priest," she said. "I have heard of you."

"I'm flattered."

"People told me, he is very tall —too tall to be a priest. You look tall—even sitting down."

"I'm secretly a basketball player pretending to be a priest," he said, thinking it sounded a bit lame, but she laughed softly and smiled.

"I can believe it," she said. "How are you, Father?"

"I'm okay. But I'm not a priest."

"No?"

"I just work for the church. Call me Donovan."

"Not Father?"

"I'm too tall for that – remember?"

"I do. You have a sense of humor. I imagine that has been useful here in Les Cayes lately."

Donovan nodded and had fleeting images of the dead in the riot.

"You're not from Les Cayes?"

"Port-au-Prince," she said. "But my family has a house here. For vacations."

"May I ask your name?"

"Emmanuella," she said. "Emmanuella Calezar."

"That's very lovely."

"You're very kind, Donovan."

"Kindness has been in short supply lately," he said. "I'm trying to make up for it."

"There will be times better than these. I feel it."

He raised his beer to her.

"I hope so. How long have you been in Les Cayes?"

"I arrived a few days ago."

"You missed all the excitement, then."

"But *you* saw it up close, I imagine."

"Yes. I did. I wish I hadn't." He looked off at the Caribbean for a moment. "Did you hear about it in Port-au-Prince – before you came down?"

"Yes," she said. "I was not sure I really wanted to come, but my mother wanted to and I wanted to be with her."

"Just you and your mother?"

"My father, too. He has business in Port-au-Prince but likes to get away from it in Les Cayes."

"What about your husband?"

"I am not married, Donovan."

He didn't know what to say and glanced again at the Caribbean.

"So, what is the latest news from Port-au-Prince, Emmanuella?"

She shrugged her shoulders.

"The news is always Baby Doc this, Baby Doc that. Will he go, or will he stay? The Americans want him to go, but that is a delicate matter, I suppose."

Donovan finished his beer.

"What do you think of Baby Doc, Emmanuella?"

"I think it is risky to talk about Baby Doc in public."

He nodded.

"It can be. Fatal, too."

"I can trust you to be discrete?" she said.

"Of course. I'm not a priest, but I *am* tall – remember?"

"I am sorry for what happened here," she said. "A disgrace."

"Does your family know Baby Doc—in Port-au-Prince?"

"My father has met him."

"And you?"

"Yes—once. Quite briefly. At a reception. My father has a large exporting business. It's inevitable to mingle sometimes with the government."

"Mingling with Baby Doc—was that, pleasant?"

She frowned.

"It was necessary. No more than that."

He sensed she did not like Baby Doc at all, likely found him quite distasteful, and was simply reluctant to say too much publicly. That was prudent, wise.

"I'm sorry," Donovan said. "I think I ask too much of you."

"No, you do not. There are more pleasant topics, though."

"Like the food, for example," Donovan said. "I never thought I'd like rice and beans so well. And I love the red snapper here, too."

"You should try Diri ak djon djon sometime – rice in black mushroom sauce," she said.

"I will look for it somewhere. What's the secret to Haitian cuisine, Emmanuella?"

"Epis," she said. "Sauce from peppers, garlic, and herbs such as thyme. Parsley, too."

"On fish as well?" he said.

"Certainly," she said. "Tonight at my house we have red snapper. And yellowtail and conch fritters and fried bananas."

"That's a feast," Donovan said. "I envy you."

"You don't have to envy us. Would you like to join us?"

"I wouldn't want to impose."

"But you would not," she said. "You are welcome."

"Really? But I'm a stranger. What would your parents say?"

"My father would no doubt ask you about events here in Les Cayes. You would be very welcome. My parents are friendly people. My father grew up poor but made something on his own."

"Then I must do it," Donovan said, "because I have never had fried bananas."

"You live a sheltered life, I think."

"Not as much as you think," he said, almost wishing he could share all he knew about rebels and soldiers and Gilles and the CIA.

"We shall treat you, then," she said. She wrote an address on a piece of paper and handed it to him.

"Shall we say eight o'clock, Donovan?"

"We shall. Until then."

"Until then," she said standing and offering her hand. They shook hands lightly and her hand felt warm and soft. She smiled and turned away and he watched her until she went out of sight. On the way home he stopped at the bar Gilles frequented and asked the bartender if Gilles had been in, but the old man merely nodded no slowly and finished wiping a glass clean. Donovan went home and took a nap before cleaning up for dinner.

Chapter Six

The Calezar home was outside Les Cayes toward Saint-Louis-du-Sud and overlooking Baie de Cavailon. There was a gentle, caressing Caribbean breeze when he arrived just before eight. He wore his cleanest white shirt, khaki slacks, and his white linen jacket. His hair had grown out a bit and he combed it into shape as best he could. And he had thought to bring a large scarlet Hibiscus plant he hoped would perhaps brighten a room and please Emannuella and her mother, and demonstrate that he was a man of quality to the father. Or at the very least, thoughtful.

The father, he felt, would respect him as the church's local representative and want to discuss politics and local news. It would be a good business strategy to have a connection to the church through a young American. And it sounded as if the red snapper and yellowtail would be exquisite. All in all, Donovan felt it beat the hell out of watching soldiers toss bodies into a truck. Or cryptic conversations with Gilles.

Emmanuella answered the door.

"Well, a gift. What shall we make of this?"

"It's just a plant."

"I tease," she said, "because you are so good about it."

"Haiti has helped me grow a thick skin," he said, holding up the plant. "I was told the hibiscus is the unofficial flower of Haiti. Or is it official?"

She accepted the flower.

"It is officially beautiful—how about that?"

"We have a winner. But I'm early. I hope you don't mind."

"You are right on time," she said, showing him in and through the extensive foyer. "Are you sure you don't want me to call you Father, though?"

"And ruin a perfectly good evening?"

She smiled.

"Would that truly ruin anything?"

"No, not at all. I think nothing could."

They walked through a large living room out to a spacious veranda overlooking Baie de Cavalion. The water was very blue and calm. A breeze ruffled his hair playfully. Emmanuella's parents were sitting at a table. Her mother was named Fabiola, an attractive woman in her late fifties – an older version of Emmanuella. The father, Pierre-Louis, was handsome, white-headed, and nearly as tall as Donovan. The father rose and walked toward them with a smile.

"I am Pierre-Louis," he said. "But Pierre is fine."

Donovan accepted the firm handshake.

"Welcome, Donovan," Fabiola said.

"A pleasure to know you, Mrs. Calezar."

Emmanuella placed the hibiscus on a table.

"Donovan brought us a beautiful hibiscus," Emmanuella said.

"Very practical," Pierre said. "We can snip a few leaves to garnish drinks."

"I didn't know that was done," Donovan said. "I learn more about Haiti every day."

"And *we* seem to learn more about Haiti every day," Pierre said. "I am truly saddened by recent events in Les Cayes."

Donovan nodded but was not sure what to say. There was an awkward silence and Fabiola broke it:

"The hibiscus leaves also have healing properties," she said. "It is said they can cure many things."

"Can they cure us of Baby Doc?" Donovan said, immediately worrying it was too much to say to strangers, and in their own home. He glanced at Emmanuella but thankfully saw no signs of reproach in her face. She appeared interested in hearing the reaction from her parents.

"It will take far more than hibiscus leaves," Pierre said. "And many will die in the effort."

"Many have already died," Donovan said. "But I think I'm being rude to bring this up here in your home. I apologize."

"No need," Pierre said. "This household has no true loyalty to Baby Doc. He is repugnant."

"Emmanuella tells me you met him."

"Yes," Pierre said. "A conference of business leaders last year in Port-au-Prince."

"What was he like?"

"A cordial enough monster," Pierre said.

"That makes him even scarier. We tend to prefer our human monsters to foam at the mouth -- like Hitler, I suppose."

"He is a Hitler, make no mistake," Pierre said. "On a smaller scale."

"Such talk at dinner," Fabiola said gently. "I don't disagree, but perhaps we should eat dinner now and enjoy the evening."

"I second that," Emmanuella said.

"Are you hungry, Donovan?" Pierre said.

"Famished. But I confess I've already had red snapper for lunch."

"Then it will be yellowtail for you," Fabiola said.

After dinner, the rainy season finally started, and the rain was initially thick and quite constant. Donovan sat over coffee with Emmanuella in the shelter of an awning on the veranda. It was after ten o'clock and her parents had gone to bed.

"I don't mean to pry," he said. "But what do you do in Port-au-Prince?"

"I have several shops," she said. "Clothing, mostly. But also tourist products."

"Are your shops closed now?"

"I have good managers," she said. "At least I hope I do."

"Business is good?"

"It will be better when Baby Doc goes."

"You say that as though it's certain."

"Eventually I think it must be so, Donovan. America would like him to go. America has a way of getting what it wants."

"Not always. Let's hope this time, though."

The rain picked up again.

"I think you will have to swim home in this rain, Donovan."

"Maybe I should just jump in the bay and let the current take me around to Les Cayes. It's only two miles – and I won't be any wetter, will I?"

"Likely not," she said. "The rainy season held off a bit longer this season. Now it is here to stay a while."

"But now I won't have to walk back – I can float."

She laughed.

"I would loan you a surfboard if we had one."

"If you have an umbrella I can borrow, I'll be fine."

"That I can arrange," she said. "But you must have more coffee before you go – to keep you warm and energetic."

She took their cups inside, filled them, and came back with an umbrella under her arm.

"I should start back soon," Donovan said. "It'll be after midnight when I get back."

"Finish your coffee first. And tell me about being mistaken for a priest in Haiti."

"Not much to tell, really."

"And yet I know that's not so."

He smirked.

"I guess it's a bit disingenuous of me to claim there's nothing to say after what's happened, isn't it?"

"I don't know," she said. "It is natural to want to forget it, I guess."

"I never will."

"No. Who could?"

"Baby Doc?"

"Baby Doc is far from here now, Donovan."

"And yet closer than we all realize."

After a minute Emmanuella said, "Do you like your job here?"

He needed a few seconds to answer:

"I like helping people. I think I always have."

"That's a safe answer."

"It's a job," he said after a moment. "Rome pays me, and

I show up."

"Spoken like a man who has grown weary of his job."

"Perhaps. I suppose I didn't bargain for the violence."

"Where are you from, Donovan?"

"Michigan. A small town up north—Mancelona."

"It is a lovely name, Mancelona. It is like the name of a beautiful woman."

"Emmanuella is a better name, for a beautiful woman."

She glanced down briefly, and he hoped he had not embarrassed her, or had violated etiquette.

"Now I know why Rome pays you to show up, Donovan – you are a diplomat."

She smiled and he felt better.

"There's precious little diplomacy happening around here," he said. He drank the last of his coffee and sat the cup on a table. "And now I must swim home."

He stood, and as she stood, too, he extended a hand to help her. She squeezed his hand, and he felt a little embarrassed and thrilled at the same time. She walked him to the door and handed him the umbrella.

"With my luck, there's a hole in it," he said, laughing nervously.

"It's a new one. I brought it from Port-au-Prince. It will see you home."

"Thanks," he said. "And thank your parents again for me – dinner was amazing."

"You will come back?" she said. "For another dinner?"

"I'd love to."

"Then, be well, Donovan from Mancelona, and stay as dry as you can."

He opened the umbrella and stepped out from under the front door awning.

"No leaks," he said. "So far."

"See? You can trust me."

He wondered if that was true. He wanted it to be true. He was learning not to assume. Haiti was a minefield wrapped inside a jungle overlooking the sparkling sea.

"And you can trust me to bring your umbrella back."

"I will hold you to that," she said, smiling.

Donovan waved and then headed down the drive to the road in the thick rain. The umbrella kept him dry at first, but the wind whipped up the rain and pelted him. It was nearly 1 am when he got home, thoroughly drenched. He stripped off his clothes, dried himself, laid down on his bed naked, and watched a large moth crawl across the ceiling, then he fell asleep and slept quite well.

Chapter Seven

Two days after dinner with the Calezars, Gilles showed up at the little church as Donovan tried to nap on his bed but could not quite fall asleep and was anyway happy to listen to the rain hammer the roof. Gilles knocked on his door but came in before Donovan could invite him. He made his way into the bedroom, pulled up a dining table chair, and sat next to the bed.

"Well, come on in, Gilles," Donovan said, still staring at the ceiling and enjoying the rain.

He wondered vaguely where the moth had gone.

"Are you sick, Donovan?"

"Nope. Just listening to the rain and taking it easy."

"I see." Gilles glanced up at the ceiling. "And do you get inspiration from the ceiling?"

"I'm listening to the rain, Gilles."

"Ambitious."

"Haven't you ever just stopped everything you're doing and listened to it rain?"

"Lately my life has been too busy for such things."

"You really should give it a try."

"I will place it on my list of things to do."

"Is it a long list?"

"There is not enough paper to complete it."

"You have a complicated life, Gilles."

"No doubt.

Is church business so slow you take naps during the day?"

"Is CIA business so slow you disappear for days on end?"

"That is when it is busiest."

Donovan swung his legs off the bed and sat up facing Gilles.

"Is something happening, Gilles?"

"Lunch is happening. We should have some."

"You're here to take me to lunch?"

"Would you be happier if I drug in several wounded men and let them bleed on your bed?"

"Do you have some with you?"

"No—no wounded men today. Maybe tomorrow."

"Well, at least that would be the Gilles I know best."

* * *

There was a lull in the rain, and they ate lunch at the beach, at the same place where Donovan had met Emmanuella. After a lunch of riz djon-djon – rice and mushrooms – along with red snapper, they drank another round of Prestige lager.

"So, Donovan – did you hear anything useful when you talked with the soldiers?"

"They like rum."

"They're Haitian. Of course they like rum. Anything else?"

"One of them told me he misses a certain lady in Port-au-Prince very much. And his mother, too. But not quite as much as the certain lady in Port-au-Prince."

"I see. With intelligence such as this, how can the rebels lose?"

"I said I'd be your stoolie, Gilles. I didn't promise to be named stoolie of the month or ferret out the location of Baby Doc's secret nuclear program."

"He does not have one of those," Gilles said.

"See—there's some intelligence we can be thankful for."

"As a stoolie, you make a better priest, Donovan."

"Sorry, but I somehow missed Spying 101 when I was in college."

"As secretive as the church can be, I should think all its employees are natural spies," Gilles said.

"I'm neither a natural spy nor a natural pretend priest, Gilles."

"Have you had an epiphany, Donovan?"

"Facing facts, I guess."

"Would you like a different line of work?"

"A promotion from stoolie? I hadn't dared hope for such a thing."

"Good," Gilles said. "You still have a sense of humor. Useful to have these days."

"What sort of work, Gilles?"

"A liaison. A go-between. For times when I am unavailable."

"Just how does that work?"

"You would be someone the rebels can meet with to know what the soldiers are doing, where they go. Things such as that."

"Still sounds like a stoolie," Donovan said. "Do I at least get a pay raise?"

"You are not being paid, remember?"

"Well, then how about a medal?"

"We do not do these things for medals."

"What *do* we do them for, Gilles?"

"We do them to make things right."

"Oh, I see—setting things right. How idealistic."

Gilles chuckled.

"You are a more natural spy than you think."

"Yeah? How so?"

"You have the requisite cynicism, for example. And suspicion."

"Maybe I should have gone to school at Langley instead of Michigan State."

"I can put in a good word for you if you like," Gilles said. "I know people."

"I bet you do. So, what's the drill for this liaison job?"

"Someone comes to you from time to time. They ask what you know."

"That's it?"

"It is truly that simple, Donovan."

"Sounds *too* simple. "

"Simplicity is good in a revolution."

"So, what's the catch?"

"The same as for anyone in this business – never have anyone know who you really are, or what you really are doing."

"Sounds risky and the pay is low, too."

"There is no pay, remember?"

"A guy can dream, can't he?"

"But you are paid in satisfaction, Donovan."

"Well, then I guess it's good that my overhead is pretty low these days."

"A mature attitude."

"And someday, when this is all over, I'll look back on it all with – great satisfaction?"

"Let us hope so, Donovan. If we get to look back someday, that will be considerable payment in itself."

"That's some sales pitch, Gilles."

* * *

From lunch at the beach, they walked back through town to the church. The rain picked up again. It fell hard.

"I have to disappear once more," Gilles said.

"How long?"

"Just for a day or so. And you can go back to your nap."

"The Life of Riley, here in Les Cayes."

"You are becoming an optimist, Donovan."

"Reluctantly. So, where are you going?"

"You do not want to know."

"And I don't want to know what you'll do there, right?"

"You learn quickly, my friend."

"A stoolie has to be fast on his feet, Gilles."

"Liaison."

"Oh, right," Donovan said.

"Stoolie sounds... vulgar."

"We wouldn't want any vulgarity in the middle of a revolution, Gilles."

"Not at all. There are standards."

"One more thing, Gilles."

"Yes?"

"*Are* we friends?"

"We certainly are not enemies."

"Is that a yes?"

Gilles shrugged but smiled. He had teeth a dentist could

admire.

"Who knows where it might go from here."

Chapter Eight

At first, Donovan wondered whether the lack of people coming to see him at the church was because he was often seen talking to soldiers in town. Was he viewed by locals as a turncoat? And he certainly couldn't tell anyone that he was actually trying to spy on the soldiers to help the rebels. Also, he began to wonder if Gilles was just playing a joke on him, and he wasn't really his stoolie or liaison or whatever, and that no one from the rebels would be coming to see him.

And he quickly decided he was okay with the lack of visitors. It gave him more time to lay in his bed listening to the rain and then eating red snapper and beans and rice washed down with beer at the beach when the rain let up. Eating well was one of the few things reliably good in Haiti. It certainly wasn't what Rome would envision him to be doing, but Rome wasn't around and that was that. He was on his own and this was what it looked like.

Nothing much was happening in Les Cayes at all. The soldiers had become predictable and stayed close to food centers and their barracks and at night sometimes drank rum on the beaches. They had even stopped firing into the air and the surf. And if the rebels were still in the hills beyond the town, they were awfully quiet, too. He knew, of course, that if some of them came down from the hills to see the town for themselves they would do so quietly, unobtrusively, and simply blend in.

But if they did come down occasionally, shouldn't one of them come by the church and sort of check-in and give him a knowing wink or slap him on the back and call him comrade, or comrade padre, or father comrade padre? And if they actually did sometimes sneak into town for a look-see, why did Gilles need him as a stoolie? He made a note to ask Gilles next time if it really was all just a shitty little CIA prank.

* * *

Two days after Gilles disappeared again, Donovan had gone to the beach to eat and drank three Prestige lagers *and* a shot of Rhum Barbancourt and badly needed the walk home to sober up. When he got back to the church there was a boy of perhaps seventeen waiting to see him. One of the rebels, Donovan speculated. Too young for that, he hoped, and the boy turned out to just be a local boy who wanted to talk, and his English was quite good.

They sat in two old wooden chairs outside the church. Donovan knew it would start raining again soon and that would be an easy way to end the conversation and go inside to nap again. He looked up at the sky: quite promising, he thought.

"How are you, Father?" the boy said. Donovan had not been called Father in earnest by anyone in some time. It sounded odd to him.

"I'm well, son." Or as well as he felt he could expect

after three beers and a shot of Rhum Barbancourt. "And you, son?"

"Good, Father. Thank you for asking."

"Part of the job," Donovan said. He knew better than to protest that he was not a priest. Nobody accepted that and it was pointless to try anymore. He really wished he could go inside and take a nap.

"Not so many people come to the church lately," the boy said.

"Maybe it's all this rain," Donovan said, glancing again at the dark sky.

"Maybe," the boy said. "Maybe people have lost faith."

Donovan really didn't want to have to talk about faith. That was not his department.

"What makes you think so, son?"

"There is much uncertainty," the boy said.

"About what, son?"

"People do not know what will happen next."

"The very definition of uncertainty."

Donovan was hoping that what happened next involved rain, his bed, and a nap.

"People are worried, Father."

"Well, I wouldn't fret too much. All will be fine, I'm sure, son."

"Are you really sure, Father?"

"Of course. Have you prayed lately, son?"

"I have, Father."

"Excellent. Keep doing that."

That sounded pretty priestly, he felt. All he had to do was adequately reassure the boy and see him on his way and then he could hit his rack just in time for the rain.

"Do you know what will happen next, Father?"

"More rain, I suspect. Perhaps tomorrow, too."
"I do not mean that, Father. With the rebels, I mean."
"I'm afraid I don't know the rebels, son."
"You don't?"
"No. So I can't know what they will do."
"Should I join the rebels, Father?"
Donovan arched his eyebrows dramatically.
"That's not for me to say, son."
"I see," the boy said. "I thought you might have an opinion."
"Do you *think* you should join the rebels, son?"
"I do not know."
"Well, if it's not clear to you, then perhaps you should give it more thought."
"Thank you, Father."
"And of course, pray often."
"How often?"
"Whenever you can."
"I will, Father. Thank you for listening."
"I'm always here, my son."
But quickly after the boy had gone, Donovan realized he was barely there at all.

Chapter Nine

The next day, a Saturday, Donovan forced himself to get up early instead of lingering in bed and staring at the ceiling. He bathed and shaved, put on a clean shirt, and took a walk to get himself going. He stopped for coffee in town and then walked back to the church and made himself a breakfast of spaghetti and watercress flavored with epis – a gift from the mother of the young boy killed in the riot. He had gone to her house and prayed with her, and she had seemed to appreciate it greatly. He was enough of a pretend priest that he could comfort someone.

Spaghetti for breakfast took some getting used to, but it was quite good and hardy, and Donovan had learned it was a common Haitian breakfast food. He ate slowly at his tiny table in his bedroom. It was very quiet in his room. The walls were bare, and he wondered whether he should put up a picture or two.

He almost wished Gilles would burst in with the latest clandestine patter. Back in Michigan – if it was breakfast time, that is – his parents would be having bacon and eggs and whole wheat toast with butter and grape jam and orange juice, and his mother would regale his father with what she had planned for the day. His father, he speculated, might actually like spaghetti for breakfast. His mother might view it as borderline heathen, though she did have some Italian blood.

He missed his parents, but not in a desperate way. He did not long for their help, for example. What good would that do? He knew he had gotten himself into his present circumstances, and he had to be the one to get himself out.

How to do that was not at all clear to him. And now he was riding on the back of the tiger in his association with Gilles and the rebels. But he would write his parents another long letter soon and let them know he was just fine and helping people and eating strange but wonderful new foods and broadening his horizons. A fairy tale.

After breakfast, he made his bed for the first time in a while, and he wiped off the table and washed dishes in the tiny sink. Sitting outside in a chair, he made a vow not to drink on this day. He would keep the vow several days a week, at least. Maybe more. He would sometimes have a drink as a reward of sorts and not as a habit. He would do laundry more often and try to always have a clean shirt to wear, even if it meant washing one in the tiny kitchen sink. He would try to shave every day, though he did not think that missing a day here and there was so bad. And he knew he would sometimes miss a day.

But he would introduce some discipline back into his life wherever he could. There was no point in falling apart if one still had the gumption to avoid it. He was the pretend American priest in Les Cayes, and regardless of his feelings about letting people call him priest, he would outwardly, at least, maintain a semblance of the image. There would be dignity to be had in such a routine.

Donovan even lingered around the church for a few hours, sitting outside in some shade to show he was there – the pretend priest was in and open for business – but no one came by. He snacked on some pikliz, a spicy slaw of carrots, cabbage, and peppers in spices that the mother of the dead boy had also given him. He momentarily wished he had a Prestige lager to wash it down with but quickly remembered his vow and drank some milk.

Then he slipped on his loafers and walked through town again to the beach. There was enough spaghetti and pikliz left for his dinner, so he decided he would avoid his favorite beach café on this day and instead walk the beach and the promenade of shops and stores. The extra exercise would increase his appetite and help awaken him from lethargy.

He walked along the beach and in the surf carrying his loafers and nodded when he saw someone who looked familiar and stopped once to chat briefly with a store owner along the promenade who swept the sidewalk in front of his shop. It was a short, superficial conversation about the weather and sales of t-shirts and such, but friendly, and Donovan encouraged the man and his wife to stop by the church sometime and the man said that would be agreeable, but Donovan knew he probably wouldn't. But he had maintained the image, and someone would either come by the church or not and his conscience would be clear either way.

He had walked quite far, farther than on most days, but he felt good from it and better about himself for having done it and for demonstrating some discipline. He sat at a table on the beach promenade and drank a coffee from a nearby stand and watched people go by and for a little while did not much think about rebels in tall green hills beyond the town, or smarmy and mysterious CIA agents or the mothers of dead children.

He cherished the sound of surf and drank a second coffee. There was a moment as he sat there – not an epiphany – and more just a gradual realization that finally slipped into place, that he was no longer the raw and fresh kid from Michigan who had entered a seminary, much to his own surprise as anyone else's, and then had gone onto Rome because he could somehow pass each test along the way. He had seen too much to be that boy anymore. And he knew he had gone further into the priesthood than he was supposed to go. It was that simple, really.

It wasn't that he lacked ability. He knew the prayers and the concepts and had the capacity for compassion and empathy and truly did enjoy helping people. But he lacked the dogmatic conviction. He was not a conservative man. He believed in God. He had that faith. But he did not now see himself as capable of being merely one of God's servants – a Christian soldier, as he often heard it termed as a boy. A paragon of virtue, his mother once said. He was just a man. He was beginning to understand his limitations, his flaws, as well as his strengths. Some were called to the priesthood and Donovan never was. He snuck in the back door and somehow made it to the parlor through determination and hard work. Had it been mostly just a challenge? Perhaps. To some degree, certainly.

A silly but apt example came into his mind: Robert Vaughan's character in *The Magnificent Seven*, a man who desperately wanted to be perceived as a ruthless gunfighter, and who, at the crucial moment of being tested, succumbed to fear and mental paralysis and failed to become his dream.

Donovan had not failed, actually. At his moment of being tested, the riot in Les Cayes, he had more or less endured; and he found the capacity to comfort people after an initial period of fear and revulsion. He was competent enough at his job, just lacking in the conviction, zeal, and indefatigable desire to make it a lifetime of service. He now knew this and it was the first time the realization was as clear to him as the horizon was out in the Caribbean.

He needed to stand and felt a burden had been lightened. Perhaps not the entire load, to be sure, but enough to lighten his burden and make a difference. He stepped back onto the beach and stood in the shade of a palm tree, its fronds whispering above him in a breeze, as he looked out over the Caribbean and felt some pangs of regret but also quite good after a few minutes and pleased to have reached a sense of understanding of who he was.

He looked back to the promenade and saw Emmanuella and she waved to him. She looked lovely, and her tan skin a warm contrast with a white skirt and aquamarine top. She did not wear a hat this time, and her dark long hair danced on her brown shoulders. He joined her on the promenade at a café's table. She drank coffee and Donovan chose tea.

"I see you did not drown the other night," she said.

He laughed.

"It was quite a swim home. I swear I was followed by a shark at one point."

"Did you give him a sound slap on the snout with your umbrella?"

"No need – I used the umbrella as a boat and floated away from him."

"Very resourceful, Donovan. A skill learned at seminary?"

"No. No, these days my skills are Haitian."

"How mysterious."

"Not at all."

"I'm sure I don't know what you mean," she said.

"I meant only that I've learned much here in Haiti."

"I'm sure you have."

"More than people know, Emmanuella."

"More mystery."

"Not so much."

"I think you are a man of mystery, Donovan."

"Just a man. I have lately come to know that."

"A good man, Donovan?"

"I believe so, yes. But mostly just a man, and not a paragon of virtue," he said, recalling what his mother had once said defined a priest.

"Are these thoughts sudden?" she said.

"They've been coming for some time. Now they've arrived."

"It sounds ominous."

"No—not at all. It's – liberating."

He felt her looking at him as he sipped his tea and glanced out at the Caribbean. He had said out loud what was in his head and heart and felt quite good about it. He felt relieved and even almost peaceful. It felt awfully good to finally meet himself.

Chapter Ten

The next evening, Donovan went to dinner at Emmanuella's. Her parents had gone up the coast for a couple days, to Jacmel, to visit friends. The rain had abated when he walked out to the house, and Donovan hoped rather than prayed that his luck would hold for the return trip. Emmanuella poured a glass of French Bordeaux for each of them, and they sat in the shade of a palm on the veranda overlooking Baie de Cavailon.

Donovan offered a toast: "To the end of Baby Doc."

"Let us hope," she said, touching her glass to his.

They drank silently a moment, and Donovan looked out over Baie de Cavailon. He could thank his time as a pretend priest for allowing him to see such great beauty. It also made him think of Lake Michigan in summer. He would like to see the Great Lake again sometime. No one was shooting rioters on Lake Michigan. No rebels in the hills. It was all quite civilized there. And likely the CIA had little interest in Michigan.

And he had aged. He could see it in the mirror when he shaved: the soft lines of boyhood had given way to harder angles.

"Are you off somewhere," Emmanuella said.

He smiled sheepishly.

"I was out there, in the middle of the bay. It's so beautiful. If this were my house I'd want to sleep on the veranda and smell the Caribbean."

"Were you on a boat or swimming in your daydream?"

He looked out at the bay again.

"I must have been on a boat because I had my wine glass, and I was listening to waves."

"A lovely dream, Donovan."

"No need to dream – it's all right there."

"Will dinner be able to compete, I wonder?"

"Depends on what dinner is."

"I am not so gifted a cook as my mother. But I can manage. Tonight—flounder and fried sweet potatoes. A light salad, too. How does that sound?"

"It sounds great. Worth the hike out here, for sure."

"You are athletic. I think you enjoy hiking."

"I do. Back home, I used to hike along Lake Michigan."

"I have been to America – once," she said. "Miami."

"That's one America," he said. "Michigan is another."

"Oh? How so, Donovan?"

"Michigan is less glamorous than Miami. Very cold and snowy in the winter. But moderate and sunny in the summer. Miami is more like here but with better everything. That sounds dumb, I know."

"Do you miss Mancelona?" she said.

He mulled it and sipped his wine. Looking out over Baie De Cavailon, Michigan seemed as far as the dark side of the moon.

"I would enjoy seeing my parents. It's been a few years. But I don't miss Michigan as I did when I first was in Rome.

I guess we get used to where we end up and adjust to how it's often far from where we started. But that's drifting into philosophy and not suitable dinner talk."

"There are no dinner conversation rules here," she said.

He smiled and raised his glass to her.

"What are your parents like?" she said.

"My mother is a firm Catholic."

"How firm?"

"Strident, I would say."

"She must be proud of you."

He looked back out into the bay. It was nearly mesmerizing.

"A few years ago, when I attended seminary – yes. She could not quite believe her good fortune to have a son try to become a priest."

"And your father? Was he pleased?"

Donovan laughed softly.

"I think he was confused."

"He did not approve?"

Donovan shook his head.

"It wasn't that. But he was surprised."

"Why?"

"He goes to Mass because my mother expects it. He would not go on his own. He fixes cars and likes a world free of as many doctrines as possible."

"I see," she said. "My father is similar, but he does go to Mass, too. Does your mother work?"

He nodded.

"In the library at one of the schools."

"When will you see them again?"

He shrugged.

"I don't know. I don't even know how much longer I'll

be in Haiti."

"Do you like Haiti?"

"Which Haiti?" he said. "The one with soldiers and riots and Baby Doc? Or the one with exquisite food and Caribbean breezes and modest people just trying to live their lives?"

"There is only one and true Haiti," she said. "It will flourish again when Baby Doc is gone."

"Here's to that," he said, raising his glass to her again. "Sorry to have been so serious."

"A pretend priest must often be serious."

Far out in Baie de Cavailon, a fishing boat was a small speck chugging along, and he watched it for a few moments.

"Do you often befriend pretend priests, Emmanuella?"

"You are my first."

"Why me?"

"You were funny that day I met you at the beach. I liked you right away."

"As a funny pretend priest or as a funny man?"

She sipped her wine.

"I do not think I thought of it then as a choice."

"And now?"

"Do I face a choice?"

"We all face choices. I have had to choose lately."

"What choice have you made?"

He finished his wine and eased back in his chair. When he glanced out into the bay, the fishing boat was out of sight.

"A selfish one, in a way. But sometimes selfish choices are appropriate. We do the best we can with what we are. And sometimes we compromise or make practical decisions we feel we have to make. Ideology is a fine thing at times, but we can't live a life every day tucked neatly inside the purity of ideology – though Republicans in America certainly do. I'm not conservative. I can't live that way."

"We are talking politics, Donovan?"

"No, not at all." He laughed. "We're talking life. Day-to-day life. What it takes to live day to day. Maybe I'm even talking about happiness."

"Are you happy?"

"No." He was surprised at how quickly and emphatically he said it.

"What would make you happy?"

He stood up and walked to the edge of the veranda and looked out into the bay but was not looking at anything in particular. His gaze reached the horizon and would have gone further if it could. He turned back to her.

"Happiness isn't an ideology," he said. "It's just a feeling. And maybe the secret of life. I like helping people. I thought I would find happiness through the church, through helping people. But it's not for me. I thought I could make myself a part of it. But it's too grand and too dogmatic of a vision for life. Life isn't an empire to be managed. At least, it shouldn't be. I don't want my life to be an empire."

"Very profound," she said.

He returned to his seat.

"I gave a speech."

"It was a grand one, too. And I did not want to interrupt you."

"Maybe you should have stopped me," he said, chuckling.

"Not at all."

"I probably sounded pompous."

She shook her head.

"It came from your heart. That was obvious to me."

"I guess it was."

He fiddled with his empty glass and then reached for the bottle and refilled his glass. She pushed hers toward him, and he refilled it.

"Salute," he said, raising his glass. She raised hers.

"What do we salute?"

"Baie de Cavailon, I guess. And short, long-winded speeches."

It began to rain again, but not very hard, and they moved to the table and chairs under the awning and listened to raindrops striking above them for a minute.

"So, will you stop working for the church, Donovan?"

"I think I already have," he said, draining his glass. "What remains are details."

Chapter Eleven

Donovan woke up first the next morning. Emmanuella slept beside him, her dark hair partially covering her face. He listened to her breath for a while, enjoyed the softness of her breathing, and then he slipped out of her bed, pulled on his slacks, and went into the kitchen to start coffee. He found orange juice and took a glass of it out to the veranda, sat in the shade of the palm, and gazed out at Baie de Cavailon. The water was calm and blue. He looked for fishing boats but did not see any. He felt good. Actually, he felt nearly re-born.

When the coffee was ready, he poured a cup, sat again under the palm, and sipped the hot coffee carefully. He could imagine just staying at this grand house overlooking the bay and leaving the world and its many problems behind. But that was not an option and he knew it was instead a fantasy, and the world did not revolve around fantasy except perhaps for the very rich and not pretend priests.

It was funny to think of himself that way, but it was true enough: his ability to be a pretend priest was slowly leaking out, had been leaking for some time, and he would stay afloat with it just long enough to make some sort of graceful transition. But to what? He could not just abandon ship and jump overboard — and at that point, the nautical analogy seemed very silly and tedious to him, and he shook it off and finished his coffee as it began to rain again.

He heard sounds from the kitchen but decided to wait and give Emmanuella some space at first. They had gotten a little drunk the night before on the Bordeaux, but certainly knew what they were doing, and he had no regrets. None at all. He had missed the intimacy of a woman. Their lovemaking had been energetic and a little awkward at first, but they eventually found a rhythm and pace and he was pleasantly surprised to shake the years of rust off quickly.

When he felt he had given Emmanuella enough time to be awake and comfortable he went into the kitchen. She wore a white nightgown and her breasts peeked over the top of it and he could see her nipples through the fabric. She was preparing vermicelli with spicy sausage, cherry tomatoes, and spinach — a very traditional Haitian breakfast. A breakfast an army could go to war on and still be okay by lunch. He leaned into the doorway a moment and watched her.

"If you keep watching me, you will make me nervous and I might drop your breakfast, Donovan."

She smiled and brushed her hair out of her face.

"We wouldn't want that."

"I see you made coffee," she said. "God but I needed that."

"I think we had some wine last night," he said. "Maybe a glass or two."

"Two bottles," she said. "But it was good wine."

"I guess we indulged."

"Two bottles are permissible when the wine is very

good."

He went over to her, slipped an arm around her, and kissed her lightly on the neck.

"But we managed to work off those bottles, as I recall," he said.

"I think we must have. I feel better than I expected. Now sit down outside and I will bring breakfast."

"It's more like a dinner."

"Yes – and you need your energy," she said. "You may have more work to handle yet this morning."

Donovan smiled and kissed her neck again.

"In that case, I'll be sure to eat every bite."

* * *

Donovan stayed another night with Emmanuella but walked home the next morning in light rain because her parents were due back by the afternoon. After changing into shorts and t-shirt he walked into town and found Gilles at a café.

"The prodigal pretend priest returns," Gilles said. "I looked for you yesterday, but no Donovan could be found."

Donovan shrugged.

"Did I miss a coup, Gilles?"

"You disappeared."

"You disappear, I disappear – we all disappear sometimes."

Gilles nodded.

"I guess we are both of us ghosts on occasion."

"I'm real," Donovan said. "I'm not so sure about you, Gilles. What do they call you CIA guys – spooks?"

"Do I detect a rough edge?"

"Don't call me a ghost – and don't call me a prodigal

pretend priest."

"Which do you object to most – prodigal, priest, or pretend?"

"All, actually."

"I see." Gilles studied him for a moment. "I looked for you to see if anything had been going on here while I was gone. You were – off duty, I guess."

"Something like that, Gilles. Where *did* you go, by the way?"

"Port-au-Prince."

"I won't ask what you did there."

"And I will not ask what you did here."

Donovan smirked and thought about what he had been doing with Emmanuella the past two days.

"Good," he said. "Because it wouldn't be any of your business, Gilles."

Gilles arched his eyebrows.

"My, my. What has gotten into you? Such – aggressiveness."

"Get used to it, Gilles. From here on out, I speak my mind."

Gilles nodded.

"I have no problem with that. Has Rome elevated you to bishop?"

Donovan laughed loudly.

"That's good, I admit."

"I thought you might think so."

"Rome isn't likely to elevate me anywhere, I can assure you. But Rome isn't here. I'm here."

"In the middle of a revolution," Gilles said.

"As revolutions go it might as well be Saturday night in Miami Beach, as quiet as things have been lately."

"They will not stay quiet long."

"You would know."

"*Everyone* will know soon enough."

"That's ominous enough."

"I am in the ominous business, Donovan."

"Yes, you are. But I guess I'm not. Sorry, I couldn't be more help around here, but soldiers just don't tell pretend American priests much more than how much they miss their mommies."

"You have been more useful to me than you know."

"Really?"

"Of course. Working for the diocese as your – escort, shall we call it, has been a wonderful cover for me. It enables me to come and go and no one thinks anything of it at all."

"Well, there you go," Donovan said. "Still a chance for me to yet be your human shield?"

"I hope not. But you must admit, as tall as you are, you would make an excellent human shield. I will keep it in mind."

"Something to look forward to, Gilles. I'll mention it in my next letter to my mother."

"You do that. And do you tell her how much you help the poor downtrodden of Haiti?"

"I do. Rome won't be elevating me to bishop, but I can always count on her vote."

"Your mother must be a fine woman."

"Of course she is. She raised me to be the CIA stoolie you see before you."

"Human shield – remember?"

"I'd already forgotten. Paradise has a way of doing that to people. The memory is the first thing to go."

"No, it is dignity that goes first," Gilles said. "Then memory."

"That can't be right. If someone loses memory, doesn't it follow dignity would be the next to go?"

"In America, perhaps," Gilles said. "But this is Haiti."

"I'll take your word for it, Gilles. So, is *your* mother in Paris?"

"Yes. She would like to come back here to visit, but I always tell her to stay where it is civilized until Baby Doc is no more."

"Certainly gives *you* less to worry about."

"And I am thankful for that."

"We all must be thankful for something."

"What are you thankful for, Donovan?"

It was not as easy a question as it might sound like, he realized. He sipped his coffee and watched people walk by for a moment.

"Maybe I'm thankful I've kept my sanity in all this."

"Sanity is worth keeping, Donovan."

"And I'm certainly thankful I haven't been shot while standing next to *you*, Gilles."

"Very practical."

"A new skill."

"Just what do you get out of all this, Donovan? Being in Haiti, I mean?"

Donovan shrugged and held up his empty cup when he caught the waiter's eye.

"I came here to serve, Gilles. I was *sent* here. Now, I just want to survive."

"You will go back to Rome when you can?"

"No."

"Why?"

"I'm done with Rome. I'm done with the church."

"I have been gone longer than I realized," Gilles said. "When did all of this happen?"

"Oh, it's been coming for some time, Gilles. I guess I just needed a good old revolution fueled by the CIA in a third-world country for it all to crystallize so nicely."

"We do what we can, Donovan. I can tell you who to write to in Washington if you want to thank the agency properly."

"Something to consider."

"Are you really done with the church?"

"I believe so."

"Just like that?" Gilles said, snapping fingers for emphasis.

"No. It was a long time coming, I guess."

"You quit because they sent you to Haiti?"

"I haven't quit yet. There's a process to that. I imagine it's the same with the CIA."

"Something like that," Gilles said. "The CIA sent me to Haiti, but I am not quitting."

"And why should you? You have a dandy little revolution to run here."

"I do not actually run it. I *assist* it."

"I'm sure there's a fine distinction there, Gilles."

"We are sort of in the same business. Maintaining empires. Just different empires."

"I've had enough of empires," Donovan said. "That's why I'm quitting."

"A man must know why he does something, to be sure."

"Will you know when it's time to quit the CIA, Gilles?"

"I hope so. But one never knows. Sometimes the decision is made for us."

"I made my own decision. I reached my own conclusions."

"Then perhaps it is a wise choice that you are no longer a tool of the Catholic empire, Donovan."

"I guess so. But I can't just quit. I have to make notifications. And the church took care of me for years. I can't just jump ship unceremoniously."

"To be sure, the church loves ceremony."

"I'll be keeping that to a minimum."

"Then I guess there is nothing to keep you from coming with me when I go into the hills to see the rebels," Gilles said.

Donovan stared at Gilles.

"Really?"

"Yes, of course."

"Why me?"

"You are always excellent cover. If we run into the wrong people, we can claim to work for the diocese and not the CIA. For months now our presence together has been accepted."

"Always thinking, Gilles."

"That I why I am still alive."

"So, I really am your human shield."

"It would be coarse to view it that way, my friend."

"We certainly wouldn't want any coarseness."

"Certainly not in the middle of a revolution," Gilles said.

Donovan mulled it a moment.

"When would we leave?"

"In the morning. I will come to get you."

"I'll clear my calendar of appointments."

"Will that take long?"

"I just did it. Rome will have to do without me."

"Rome has been doing without you for a long time, my friend."

Chapter Twelve

Donovan and Gilles hiked up into the green hills much of the morning before taking a break for water and hardboiled eggs Donovan had wrapped in paper. He also brought a full canteen, and Gilles had shown up with a light pack containing more water, dried herring, beans and rice, and a bottle of Rhum Barbancourt.

They took turns wearing the pack, which was not heavy, but more of an inconvenience. Before they had set off, Gilles retrieved a 9 mm pistol and several clips from the pack. He checked the safety and then tucked the pistol into the waistband of his pants and slid the clips into a pants pocket.

"For target practice?" Donovan said. "In case we get bored, right?"

"In case we get bored," Gilles said as he slipped on the pack.

"Should *I* have a gun?"

"Do you *think* you should have a gun, Donovan?"

"Too late, I guess. Unless you have a spare."

Gilles slipped off the pack, produced a small .32 and extra clip, and gave them to Donovan.

"Now you have a gun, Donovan."

"I guess I do," he said, hefting the small pistol. "Where's the safety?"

Gilles showed him.

"Slip it into a back pocket and forget about it for now," Gilles said. "No time for a crash course in how not to shoot yourself in the foot."

"Aye, my captain," Donovan said, tossing Gilles a sloppy salute.

"It is not a game, Donovan."

"I know that. Believe me. Besides, if I accidentally shoot myself, at least I can pretend to give myself the last rites."

Gilles smirked.

"It is not *you* being accidentally shot that I worry about."

* * *

They rested at an overlook, and Donovan could see Les Cayes below and the Caribbean beyond. He could see the area where the church would be, but the building was hidden by a thick grove of trees.

"I should have brought a camera," Donovan said. "Except I don't have one. All this time in Haiti, and I never thought to get one. I wonder why."

"It is the thought that counts, right?"

"So they say. It would make a hell of a picture from up here."

"Can you see your church?"

"It's not *my* church," Donovan said. "It's just a building with a cross tacked onto it."

"That could be said of any church," Gilles said.

"I suppose so. Anyway, it's not the cross that makes a church. It's the people inside."

"Profound, Donovan."

"Are you even a Catholic, Gilles?"

Gilles drank more water and then slipped the canteen back into the pack.

"Certainly I was born one," he said. "My mother – like yours – is devout."

"And your father?"

"Dead."

"Oh. I'm sorry."

"No need to be sorry. These things happen. It was years ago."

"I see. Do you ever pray, Gilles?"

"Not like you. If I pray, it is because I am conceding I might get shot. At such times, I am not worrying about my immortal soul."

"A black and white world."

"When someone is shooting at you—yes, it is very much black and white. You kill them, or they kill you."

Donovan looked again out at the Caribbean.

"Life is simple sometimes, I guess," he said. "When it's not complicated, that is."

Gilles stood up and handed the pack to him.

"Your turn. See how simple life is?"

* * *

A few hours later, Donovan remembered long car rides with his parents and said with a chuckle, "Are we there yet?"

"Soon enough," Gilles said. "Here, I can take the pack now."

They made the exchange and set off again. Donovan felt he was holding up pretty well, and Gilles seemed like a seasoned hiker who didn't tire easily.

"We must have gone pretty far," Donovan said.

"Not so far in kilometers," Gilles said. "Lots of twists and turns."

"It all looks the same."

"If we could go in a straight line on level ground, it would not be so far to Les Cayes."

"Why don't the soldiers come up here?" Donovan said.

"They are lazy. And scared. They feel more secure in town."

"And why don't the rebels come down into town?"

"We are working on that."

"Are the rebels lazy, too?"

"Not particularly," Gilles said.

"Scared?"

"Of course. Only a fool isn't afraid."

"Are you afraid, Gilles?"

"Sometimes. But I have learned that fear is useful. It helps keep you aware of what is happening."

"Makes sense. I guess."

"Are you afraid, Donovan?"

"Yes. But I feel okay, too. Why is that?"

"Each man must answer that one himself," Gilles said. "Have you ever fired a gun?"

"When I was a kid. At my cousin's farm in Kalkaska."

"Did you hit anything?"

"Some pop bottles."

"There are no pop bottles up here."

"I didn't think there would be."

*　*　*

They rested again, well up into the hills.

"Tired, Donovan?"

"I feel good, actually. I've needed this exercise for a long time."

"You are a new man, maybe?"

"Something like that. Things seem simpler up here – just walk and climb, walk and climb. Thoughts get simpler, too."

"The altitude can be – liberating," Gilles said. He offered Donovan a drink from his canteen.

Donovan took a gulp and shook the canteen to see how much was left.

"You're getting low, and I have plenty."

Donovan poured some of his into Gilles' canteen.

"Why did you decide to come along?" Gilles said.

"There's no health club to join in Les Cayes."

Gilles smiled broadly.

"Your sense of humor is improving."

"I'm a work in progress. But I don't know why I came, exactly. It just seemed like the right thing to do."

Gilles nodded. After a moment he said, "Can you use that gun if you have to?"

Donovan retrieved the .32 from his pocket and looked at it.

"I don't know."

"You will know if the time comes."

"Are you so sure?"

"Certainly I am hopeful," Gilles said, grinning.

Donovan grinned back.

"Maybe we just have a picnic while we're up here, Gilles."

"Maybe."

They ate some of the dried herring in silence. After they were finished, Donovan said, "I should confess something."

"A priest confessing – how delightful," Gilles said. "And ironic – even for a *pretend* priest."

"I'm a pretend priest in name only now. Keep that in mind."

"I will try. What do you confess?"

"You asked where I was for a few days. Well, I was with a woman."

Gilles smirked.

"Father Donovan is full of surprises."

"No more Father Donovan, Gilles."

"Agreed. Can I assume that you were not being a pretend priest while you were this woman?"

"You may assume I slept with her because I did. Several times."

"Bravo, Donovan. And I thought you lived a boring life. Who is she?"

"Just someone from Port-au-Prince."

"You went to Port-au-Prince?"

Gilles sounded concerned.

"No. She is vacationing in Les Cayes – visiting her parents from Port-au-Prince. They have a vacation home on Bai de Cavailon."

Gilles frowned.

"Rich Haitian people from Port-au-Prince?"

Donovan nodded.

"I take it they have money, yes."

"The father owns an export business in Port-au-Prince."

"The name, Donovan?"

"Emmanuella Calezar. Why do you ask?"

"I know of these people," Gilles said. "Pierre Calezar is a prominent businessman in Port-au-Prince. He must associate with Baby Doc for his business."

"He was critical of Baby Doc, Gilles. I had dinner with them. He even compared Baby Doc to Hitler."

"He plays to his audience. But the Hitler reference – a nice touch."

"He said he met Baby Doc just once."

"More than that, Donovan."

"You're sure?"

"Yes, I am sure. He must appear to be what he wants you to believe."

Donovan sighed heavily.

"Are you saying he is really on Baby Doc's side?"

"I am saying that Pierre Calezar is on his side. If Baby Doc is in power, that is who he caters to."

"Okay," Donovan said. "Okay – I get that. That's par for the course of doing business. I can understand that. But are you also saying the Calezars *support* Baby Doc?"

"I do not know that," Gilles said.

"What *do* you know?"

"The real danger here is that the Calezars associate with Baby Doc. They sometimes speak to Baby Doc and his people. The risk is that they reveal something – that they reveal *your* sentiments about Baby Doc, and that is relayed to Les Cayes. Do you see?"

"I guess I do. But are you sure about all this?"

"I am. And the woman – Emanuella? You know she is married, correct?"

"She said she wasn't."

"It seems that *all* of the Calezars have lied to you, Donovan. I have seen her husband."

Donovan was stunned. He made eye contact with Gilles but could not speak for a moment.

"You have been busy, Donovan. I suggest you do not share your... exploits with Rome."

"Not much chance of that. I should have been more aware, I guess."

"You could not know," Gilles said. "But did you ever mention *my* name to the Calezars?"

"No. Never. I'm sure of that."

"You are certain?"

"Yes. No doubt."

"Good. But still, I am associated with you."

"Do you think they're capable of..."

"Of betraying you?" Gilles said. "Of betraying me? They are rich people whose wealth depends on Baby Doc – whether they like him or not. They are capable of anything."

Donovan nodded, felt foolish, and even a little sad.

"Emmanuella," he said. "I trusted her. I don't quite understand."

"She is a rich young woman with a rich young woman's appetites, my friend."

"Is it that simple?"

"I believe so, yes."

"You're a cynic, Gilles."

"A realist. I have to be in my profession. Do not take it personally. People use each other—first law of humanity. Perhaps acquiring a pretend priest is a fantasy fulfilled for her. Who knows. But take it as a lesson learned and move on. You say you are not a pretend priest anymore—absorb the lesson like a man and move past it."

Gilles stood and handed Donovan the pack.

"And now *we* have to move on, too."

Chapter Thirteen

They reached the outskirts of the rebel camp at nightfall. Up ahead, they could see the glow from the fires, and Gilles muttered "damn" and stopped and stood for a moment with his hands on his hips before crouching down and pulling Donovan down, too.

"I have to get them out of that damn hollow," Gilles whispered. "And we must kill those damn fires."

"Why?" Donovan whispered.

"It is a perfect deathtrap. What do Americans say? Fish in a pond?"

"Fish in a barrel," Donovan whispered.

"Yes," Gilles whispered. "A barrel would be even easier."

Gilles steered Donovan behind a thick tree trunk and then pulled the 9 mm from his waistband. Donovan heard him chamber a round, and it made the hair on his neck stand up.

"What's wrong?" Donovan said. He pulled his .32 from his back pocket, but Gilles seemed to have anticipated that.

"Keep your safety on, Donovan." Gilles was in front of him, peering around from the tree trunk.

"Why?"

"So you do not accidentally shoot me in the back – that is why."

"I wouldn't."

"Not on purpose," Gilles said. "But once the bullet is out, intent becomes irrelevant."

"Damn, Gilles—you're like some Zen master of espionage."

"This is not espionage, Donovan. This is common sense – making sure the rebels do not shoot us by mistake. They are not real soldiers, like U.S. Marines. Marines would make me feel much better. Here, discipline is not good."

"And they have machine guns."

"Lots of them."

"You saw to that, I guess."

"Did you think I would equip them with water pistols? Or spears?"

"I'd rather face spears, I guess," Donovan said. "Okay, so how do we get in there without getting shot?"

"We very carefully get close enough so I can whistle three times."

"Whistle?"

"That is the arrangement," Gilles said.

"My life depends on your ability to whistle?"

"We *could* just fire some shots into the air and stand up and wave like fools, Donovan."

"Whistling is good. I'm all for the whistling strategy."

"Good choice. You are a natural for this *espionage*."

"Wait—what if they don't recognize what you whistle?"

"Then it might be better if they had spears instead of automatic weapons," Gilles said. "But they know what I will whistle -- we have used it before. And they know I am coming tonight."

"What about me? Do they know *I'm* coming?"

"No. So do not stand close to me, Donovan."

"Really?"

"I kid you. But slip your pistol back into your pocket – do not make them nervous. Some of them are just boys."

"Thanks for boosting my confidence, Gilles."

"Just think of me as a Renaissance man."

"That's not the historical period I had in mind."

They moved toward the camp, going tree to tree until Gilles reached back and halted Donovan, and then Gilles whistled three times. After a few seconds, three whistles came from the camp. And when Donovan looked around the tree again, several men carrying AKs were walking toward them. Gilles stepped out from the tree and spoke in French to the men, who slapped him on the back.

* * *

The rebels were a mix of men anywhere from sixteen to fifty. But all old enough and capable enough to carry and fire a weapon. Mostly AK-47s, but also some SKS carbines of Vietnam War vintage, all provided by the CIA—by Gilles. Donovan and Gilles sat by one of the fires, and one of the rebels, a young boy, brought him a bowl of tchaka, a stew of hominy, beans, pumpkin, and a few pieces of pork. The rebel leader, Michel, sat next to Donovan. Michel was thirty, bald, and very dark with a leathery face. He looked much older than thirty. Donovan could not help but think of Marlon Brando as Kurtz.

"How is the tchaka, father?" Michel said.

"You don't have to call me father. And the stew is delicious."

"Maybe not delicious, Father. But filling."

"You don't have to call me Father. Call me Donovan."

"Why don't we call you father?"

"I have – left the church."

"You have left the church? Why?"

"I'll tell you tomorrow."

"Why tomorrow?"

"I'm too tired now to explain it intelligently."

"I see," Michel said. "And you can just leave the church?"

"I can. I have."

Donovan finished his stew, and Michel seemed amused by it all.

"Tchaka isn't just food. Do you know that, Donovan?"

"I like it pretty well as food."

"It is also used as an offering to the Loa. Do you know the Loa, Donovan?"

"Is he a God?"

"The Loa are many and not just one. But no, they are not gods. They serve gods – Voodoo gods."

"Voodoo?"

Now I am involved in Voodoo? Donovan thought.

"Yes, Voodoo, Donovan. But even some of the Catholic saints have been adopted into Loa – Saint John the Baptist, and St. Jude. Of course, you know of these saints."

"Quite well. But I didn't know they had been adopted into Voodoo."

"A long time ago," Michel said. "As a compromise of sorts with Europeans who brought Catholicism. You did not learn this in Rome?"

"I guess I hadn't yet reached that lesson. How do you know so much about it, Michel?"

"I was a schoolteacher in Les Cayes."

"Before the revolution."

"Yes, and after, too, God willing."
"Which God?" Donovan said, grinning.
"Any and all of them," Michel said, grinning too.

Chapter Fourteen

Donovan woke up the next day under a tree. He had slept well on the bare ground and knew the hike up had worn him out enough to make him sleep deeply. He sat up and looked around; a few of the rebels stirred and made coffee while others still slept, their AKs leaning against trees or beside them on the ground. Despite the weapons, it did not feel like a military camp at all to him. It felt more like a refugee camp. Uncertainty seemed to be in the air. At least, that was what he sensed.

The young boy who had served him dinner the night before brought him breakfast – more tchaka. In daylight, Donovan could see how young the boy was, perhaps fifteen, but he smiled sweetly and revealed several gold teeth. He was grateful the boy didn't call him Father or ask to hear his confession. Donovan ate the stew and drank from his canteen and felt pretty good. He sat back against the tree in no hurry for whatever was coming next.

Gilles appeared soon. He had been with Michel scouting for a new camp.

"This place is no good, Donovan. I finally convinced Michel. This place is a killing ground."

"When do we leave?"

"In a few hours," Gilles said. "This bunch is slow. Plodding. But at least I convinced them to have some lookouts."

"They aren't soldiers. You said so yourself — I can see that when I look around. Michel was a teacher. The boy who brought my stew—likely one of Michel's students."

"That is Michel's son. And yes, also one of his students."

Donovan arched his eyebrows.

"And now he carries a machine gun."

"Part of his education."

Donovan sighed.

"We didn't have that part at Michigan State."

"Welcome to the world, Donovan."

* * *

Gilles moved the rebels to a new camp on higher ground with a good line of sight on the only avenue of approach. There was even water available in a nearby stream.

"How do they get the food up here, Gilles?"

"That is perhaps the riskiest part of it all. People in Les Cayes leave it in places below the hills, and the rebels go down at night to retrieve it."

"And the soldiers don't know. Amazing."

"So far, the soldiers have been too lazy. They prefer to stay in town. But we hear that may change."

"How so?"

"A new commander. From Port-au-Prince. Someone with more ambition."

"A Baby Doc man."

"No doubt," Gilles said.

"But the tchaka is very good up here," Donovan said.

"Tchaka is good anywhere in Haiti. It is difficult to make

bad tchaka."

"We might get tired of it, though."

"We'll go back to Les Cayes soon enough. Then you can feast on red snapper again. And Prestige beer."

"I'm okay with tchaka, Gilles. I can eat a boatload of it."

"We will make a rebel out of you yet."

"Well, when I was a kid, my mother used to say I could sometimes be a bit rebellious."

"Yes," Gilles said. "Just ask the church."

"We'll skip the church on this one, Gilles."

"You are sure of your choice?"

"I'm sure. I feel it deep inside."

"Then I think it must be correct. Bad decisions stay on the skin. Good ones reach the bone. I am happy to meet the new Mr. Donovan."

Gilles offered a hand, and Donovan took it.

* * *

The rebels settled into their new camp, and Gilles and Michel sat off by themselves in the shade of a large tree for a while talking over strategy. Donovan helped fill many canteens in the nearby stream, which was fed by runoff and was therefore clean, though Gilles gave him some tablets to put in his water and urged him to do so.

"They are used to the water," Gilles said. "You are not."

Donovan felt useful and appreciated working without having to think too much. He even learned from Gilles how to field strip and clean an AK-47. In the afternoon, he hiked far down the slope to help rebels returning with supplies. There were times, he felt, when he was not thinking much at all and instead just breathing and moving and... living.

That evening, Gilles put sentries out, far down the slope for plenty of warning, and permitted fires because the new camp was nicely shielded from easy view. The evening's tchaka was supplemented by dried herring and some fruit – mangoes and avocados. And there was a new stew – legim – a mixture of cabbage, eggplant, spinach, and watercress. Donovan noticed it was thicker than tchaka and quite good. The rebel diet was quite healthy.

After dinner, he sat at a fire with Gilles and Michel. Gilles passed the bottle of Rhum Barbancourt around.

"We ate very well tonight," Michel said, gazing into the fire. "The people have provided for us very well. But what have we done for them?"

"Gave them hope?" Donovan said.

Michel looked across the fire at him but did not betray any emotion. Gilles sipped from the rum bottle and then gave it to Donovan.

"Hope's a start, right?" Donovan said.

"It is," Michel said. "And it can be a powerful force."

"But hope is fragile," Gilles said. "Hope thrives from action."

Donovan looked at Gilles and Michel and had a fleeting image of Robert E. Lee and Stonewall Jackson sitting by a fire mulling what to do next, though that was a far different revolution. He felt like he was a major or even a colonel on Lee's staff, allowed to witness the deliberations.

"What do you say, Gilles?" Michel said after a silence of several minutes.

Gilles poked a small stick into the fire and stirred the embers.

"This new officer coming from Port-au-Prince, he will change things," Gilles said. "Once he is here and in charge, things will be different. We do not know how they will change, but they will, and thus the soldiers will no longer be as we have known them. No more predictability. And the new commander may bring more troops, too."

"What do we do?" Michel said.

Gilles poked the stick into the embers some more.

"Strike first," Gilles said. "Be the ones that cannot be predicted. Strike while we still have some advantage."

Michel nodded, but Donovan felt there was uncertainty on Michel's face. Michel turned to him.

"What do you think, Donovan?"

"I'm no soldier."

"Neither was I," Michel said. "Until I became one."

"I'm an observer here, I guess."

Donovan felt a little uncomfortable.

"Is that pistol still in your back pocket?" Gilles said.

"Yes. Of course."

"And you are in a rebel camp, with a weapon?" Gilles said.

"Yes."

"Then you are a rebel, Donovan. Like it or not."

Donovan looked at them and didn't know what to say. He hadn't really thought of it that way.

"I must have had that same look on my face, Donovan, my first day here, too," Michel said.

Donovan looked into the fire a moment and then retrieved the .32 from his pocket. He handed it to Gilles.

"Then I think I'll need a bigger gun."

"A carbine should do nicely," Gilles said.

The next morning, over a breakfast of legim and bananas, it was decided that the rebels would attempt to seize Les

Cayes before the new government commander arrived to change the equation. Donovan was given an SKS carbine and a lesson on using it from Michel and then he joined Gilles and Michel to walk down into the foothills where they could contact townspeople who served as their eyes and ears.

They hoped to learn the latest on where the soldiers were and what they were doing without actually going into Les Cayes. Gilles desperately wanted to know about the new commander, and Donovan felt that Gilles must surely be thinking of the man as his counterpart. Sort of like Lee sizing up Grant.

They hiked for several hours and then rested in the shade of a grove of trees. It had felt very odd to Donovan at first to carry a rifle. But he grew used to it and was confident he knew how to use it and could if it came to that. He hoped, anyway. Gilles and Michel carried AK-47s. Donovan wondered how many times they had used them. He wished there had been time for him to have target practice with his carbine, but Gilles would not allow it for fear it would be heard.

The shade felt good, and they kept their weapons across their laps for quick access and ate dried herring wrapped in paper and some avocado. Gilles was unusually quiet, Donovan felt. He chalked it up to worry over the coming action. Donovan had not yet asked what his role in it would be, and he tried not to think too much about it. When Gilles felt it was time to go, he didn't say anything and instead stood up and shouldered his AK, and Donovan and Michel fell into line.

Donovan was last in line and sometimes looked behind him until he reminded himself that any danger would most likely be in front of them and not behind them. Nonetheless, he felt a bit exposed at the end of their tiny column.

They crossed a stream well down from the upper hills and not far above the foothills. They stopped long enough at the stream to splash water on their heads and faces and to drink from their canteens. As they paused, Donovan thought of Lake Michigan and how different was the jungle landscape from there, though just as beautiful, just as mesmerizing in its way. But he was very aware of just how far he had traveled from Mancelona. He missed it and longed to hike along the lake again someday, but he knew not to let his thoughts settle on that desire too long and to keep his focus on what was ahead, what was right in front of him at the moment.

Not far past the stream there was a road, the only one that penetrated any distance into the hills behind Les Cayes, though calling it a road was generous and it was more a cow path that a small vehicle, such as a Jeep or small car, could barely negotiate. It was also a landmark signaling that below the road the foothills began and Les Cayes was not so far. Somewhere beyond the road, perhaps in less than a mile, was where they expected to make contact with people from the town.

The three of them emerged from the trees lining the road. Gilles and Michel carried their AKs at the ready, and Donovan belatedly brought his carbine up, too, as they stepped onto the side of the road. Before they could look both ways down the road, gunfire erupted from about forty feet to their left, and several rounds struck the tree behind Donovan as Gilles and Michel returned fire at a military Jeep and a group of soldiers.

Donovan instinctively crouched low and managed to get

off a few shots, but they were wild, too high, and Gilles and Michel killed three soldiers who had been standing by the Jeep. Something moved suddenly in the tree line behind the Jeep, and as Gilles and Michel changed clips, more gunfire came their way. Donovan fired his entire clip at the spot in the trees and silenced the firing. Michel suddenly fell to the ground with a high-pitched yelp and clutched his thigh, which was bleeding.

"Pull him off the road, Donovan," Gilles yelled as he ran to the Jeep to check it.

When Gilles returned, Donovan had Michel back into the tree line and had cut open Michel's pants leg at his thigh. Gilles examined it and then searched in his pack for a bandage.

"The soldiers – all dead," Gilles said, nearly out of breath, as he ripped open the packet containing the bandage. "You killed that last one, Donovan – in the tree line. Nice work."

Donovan looked toward the Jeep, but there was nothing to see except the bodies of three of the soldiers. Adrenaline was pumping throughout him, and he was unsure how he felt other than a sense of urgency but nothing to do about it.

"You are lucky, Michel," Gilles said as he wrapped the bandage around Michel's thigh.

"I do not feel so lucky," Michel said through clenched teeth. He tried to sit up, to look down at his thigh, but could not. He looked up at the sky, trying to manage his pain, and he moaned. He was in shock and trying to say more but unable to.

"You will be fine, my friend," Gilles said. "It is a fortunate wound."

"Really, Gilles—he's fortunate?" Donovan said. "As a doctor, you make a good spy."

"The bullet has passed clean through," Gilles said. "And missed bone. He will not die and will not lose the leg – as long as we get him help soon. So, it is fortunate. If a man must be shot, this is the way to go."

"You're sure?"

"Reasonably."

"Very inspiring, Gilles."

"Yes, I feel sure, Donovan." Gilles patted Michel's shoulder. "You will be fine, old friend."

Michel nodded.

"I trust you, Gilles."

"And you know all this how?" Donovan said.

"I have seen this before."

"I don't doubt it."

"I was a medical student in Paris," Gilles said. "Before the CIA."

"The day is full of surprises."

Gilles reached into his pack and found a morphine syrette and jabbed it into Michel's thigh.

"Soon you will sing with the birds," Gilles said to Michel. "But we must get him out of here. Someone will have heard the shots."

Across the road, Donovan suddenly saw a Haitian man peering out behind a tree, and he shouldered his carbine, but Gilles pushed it away.

"No. He is our contact, from Les Cayes."

"Good God. I nearly killed him."

"But you did not. And your instinct was correct."

Gilles waved the man across the road, and he brought two other men with him.

"This is very bad," the first Haitian man said, glancing quickly down the road at the three dead soldiers. "It was surely heard in Les Cayes. And one of them got away."

"What?" Gilles said. "Where?"

"We saw a soldier running away as we arrived," the man said. "By now he will be almost to Les Cayes. The soldiers will come."

"*Two* of them in the tree line?" Donovan said, looking up at Gilles.

Gilles nodded and looked down at Michel's wound for a moment.

"I should have got the second one, too," Donovan said.

"You did very well to get one of them," Gilles said. "We must not obsess over spilt milk." He looked at the Haitian man. "Send one of your men ahead to the hospital. Get whoever is there to meet us away from the hospital. Be very calm, very discrete."

One of the men nodded and sprinted across the road and into the far tree line out of sight.

"What's your plan, Gilles?" Donovan said.

Gilles looked at him and then at Michel.

"A good question," Michel said faintly.

"We'll get this wound closed in town and leave you at a safe house," Gilles said. "It is our only option. I will help these men take you there." He looked at Donovan. "Donovan, you must go back to the camp and let them know what has happened."

"Do you think they heard the firing, Gilles?"

"Maybe not. We are very close to town. Anyway, they must know about Michel. There is another who will take command. I'll come back as soon as I get Michel into town."

"Okay, Gilles."

"Can you get back there on your own, Donovan?"

"I believe I know the way back."

"Then go—now. I'll be back tomorrow."

Donovan stood and shouldered his carbine and looked at Gilles for a moment.

Gilles smiled.

"You did very well today, Donovan. Very well indeed."

"For a pretend priest?"

"For a man."

Donovan nodded.

"Don't get yourself shot in Les Cayes, Gilles. After all, I'm your human shield."

"No, Donovan. You are my friend."

Donavan knew it was true, and he nodded again and smiled. Then he turned and slipped back into the trees toward the rebel camp.

Chapter Fifteen

Donovan reached the stream they'd crossed on the way down. As he filled his canteen, the shock wore off and realization electrified him: he'd killed a man. And he'd done it without delay or deliberation like it was routine. He'd killed a man who perhaps had simply been peeing by the side of the road. A Haitian government soldier. A Baby Doc man. And so, a threat to the people of Les Cayes. A threat to the rebels and Gilles and Michel.

But still a man, a person. The thought overpowered him as he slipped to a knee and dropped his carbine. He was suspended like that on one knee, a hand touching the ground to prevent himself from falling over — like an injured football player. He expected to vomit but did not.

After a bit, he managed to pick up his carbine and stand again, his legs shaky, hands sweaty, and throat dry. He gulped water from his canteen and looked back toward where he had just been, but there were only trees. He slung his canteen strap over his shoulder again and then remembered to check his carbine. The clip was empty, and he replaced it with a full one and slipped the empty clip into a back pocket. The rebels would probably have use for it.

And he truly was one of them now – a rebel.

He'd killed a soldier.

He was now a soldier.

But there was no time to linger and debate it, and so as he hiked, he said a prayer for the dead soldiers and for himself, too, and then he let it go as best he could, which was slow at first. Spilt milk was what Gilles had called it. It was more than that. Far more than that.

But he accepted that Gilles was right that they must not let it slow them down or deter them. It was a harsh business he was now in, and it had few rules, and it would do no good to stop and debate the morality of it. And Gilles had been right about another thing: when it came down to killing another man before he killed you, the decision was easier to make than it sounded.

It was instinct and not intellect.

And so he kept walking.

A few hours later, one of the rebel sentries stepped from behind a tree and greeted him with a smile that quickly fell apart when he looked past Donovan and did not see Michel and Gilles. The man did not say anything as he waved him on.

Donovan walked into the rebel camp and knew he must find Michel's second in command, but he did not know who that was, so he first found Michel's son.

"I don't know your name," he said to the boy.

"Jean-Paul. Where is my father?"

"Gilles and some men took him to Les Cayes. Your father was wounded."

Jean-Paul looked down at the ground a moment and then back up at him.

"Is he dead?"

"No. Gilles says he will live. They are taking him to the hospital and then a safe house."

"How did it happen?" Jean-Paul said.

"There were soldiers. At the little road in the foothills. There was a fight and Michel was wounded – in the leg."

"Did you kill the soldiers?" Jean-Paul said.

"Yes, we did, Jean-Paul." Donovan was suddenly thankful he had not gone across the road into the tree line to see the man he had killed. He did not need the man's face following him.

"And Gilles says my father will live?"

"Yes. But one of the soldiers got away. He'll warn the rest."

"You must speak to Christophe," Jean-Paul said. "Christophe will know what to do."

* * *

"I do not know what to do," Christophe said.

That surprised Donovan, but he nodded and studied Christophe's face a moment. The man was perhaps forty. His skin was lighter than Michel's and he had hair—curly dark hair. The look on his face reflected indecision but also fear.

"What would Michel do?" Donovan said.

"He would ask Gilles."

Donovan nodded again.

"But Gilles isn't here. *You're* here, Christophe."

"I simply do not know what to do, Donovan."

Donovan looked around the camp: many of the rebels sat around talking. Most were not yet aware of what had happened to Michel. And now it was clear that Christophe was a bit paralyzed with fear and would be little or no help.

"What would you *like* to do, Christophe?"

Christophe looked away.

"I do not know."

Donovan finally reached over and patted Christophe's elbow.

"We'll figure this out together, Christophe. Have the men been fed?"

"Not yet."

"Why don't you see to that."

"Yes. Thank you, Donovan."

Donovan walked among the men and many of them looked up at him and smiled as he passed by. Others napped. It had become clear to him that this wasn't three hundred Spartans at the pass of Thermopylae.

And Christophe was no Leonidas.

Hell, even Gilles wasn't Leonidas.

But Gilles was competent and knew his business. And he wasn't here. And if things went wrong in Les Cayes, maybe Gilles didn't come back at all.

For a moment, he wondered whether the rebels would be willing to look to Jean-Paul to lead them since he was Michel's son. But that seemed like a stretch. And he didn't relish having command fall to a boy.

He sat down under a tree to contemplate it and Jean-Paul brought him a bowl of legim.

"Thanks, Jean-Paul. Do you want to sit with me?"

"Yes."

"Please do."

Jean-Paul sat down.

"Have you eaten, Jean-Paul?"

"I will after everyone else does."

"You sound like your father."

"My father is truly okay?"

Donovan realized he wanted the details, and the boy was likely fit to hear them.

"The bullet passed through the thigh cleanly, Gilles said. Did you know that Gilles once studied to be a doctor?"

"No, Donovan."

"Well, apparently, he did as a younger man."

"Gilles cared for my father?"

"He did. He bandaged the wound and gave him some morphine – no more pain, you see? Gilles says your father will not lose the leg and will walk again."

"Where is my father now?"

"Gilles and some men took him to the hospital to get the wound cleaned and stitched, I imagine. Then, I don't know—a safe house somewhere. It's a safe house because no one knows where it is except a few."

"I see," Jean-Paul said. "Did my father say anything about me?"

He looked at Jean-Paul and quickly lied:

"Yes – he did. I nearly forgot because this legim is so good. But your father told me to let you know he will be back very soon. He asked me to tell you to be brave."

"I will."

"And I will tell him so when I see him."

"When will that be, Donovan?"

"I don't know. But soon, I hope."

After he ate, Donovan rested for a few minutes and assessed things. What if Gilles didn't return? And how would the soldiers in Les Cayes react? By now, the soldier who had escaped had told them what had happened. What would they do? Until now they had shown little appetite to comb the hills after that first time beyond Bauzain, when many soldiers were killed.

But Gilles had said a new commander was coming. A man who might not be timid. And the soldiers would likely be angry now. Donovan wished he had killed that man, too, the one who escaped. But then he thought, what difference would that have made? He would have done it if he could, but it wouldn't have changed much. Michel would still be wounded, and Gilles would still have to risk his life to take him into Les Cayes. And eventually, the soldiers would know about the dead men. It would simply have been a matter of time.

Donovan tried to think like a soldier but that was not his training. And he could expect no real direction from Christophe. He got up and walked around the camp again. What did he know? Well, there were several sentries down from the camp. But that was put in place when things had been quiet and slow. Things were no longer quiet. And might speed up soon. He looked for Christophe.

"Christophe, will you be willing to send a few more men down the hill as sentries? Further down than now, I mean. We need more warning, just in case."

"I can do that, Donovan."

"Good, my friend."

He watched Christophe gather a few men. They were laughing as they picked up their AKs, and Donovan hoped that wasn't a bad sign. He decided he should go with Christophe to make sure the sentries were placed as far down as he envisioned. As he feared, Christophe wanted to merely add them to sentries already in position, not far from camp.

"Farther down, Christophe, so we have plenty of warning if someone comes."

Christophe clearly did not like the idea.

"Maybe we should move the camp, Donovan."

Donovan was growing impatient.

"Christophe, where would you suggest we go?"

"Deeper in the hills?"

"But to where? Here we have a pretty good position. There's only one way in, and we can cover that pretty well. Gilles picked this spot because it's good."

"Gilles is not here."

"But he will come back—tomorrow. He will expect us to be here."

Christophe looked at his men, who also looked uncertain.

"Okay, Donovan. We do it this way. But if Gilles does not come tomorrow, we must move."

"Fine," Donovan said. "But no fires tonight. And camp must be quiet."

"Yes," Christophe said. "Quiet as a mouse."

Donovan nodded. At least he had bought some time.

* * *

There was some grumbling about the lack of fires, but that night the rebels ate legim and tchaka and fruit and that seemed to improve their outlooks as they sat in the dark in clumps and talked quietly among themselves. Donovan sat with Jean-Paul and Christophe. After Jean-Paul went off to sleep, he produced what was left of the bottle of Rhum Barbancourt. He took a swig and handed it to Christophe, who did the same.

"We finish the rum for Gilles," Donovan said with a laugh, hoping to perk up Christophe, who was nearly sullen. "But he'll scold us for it."

"Gilles is very busy now," Christophe said. "And he can

get more rum in Les Cayes."

"I doubt he's thinking much about that now."

"No. But if he does not come back tomorrow, we must move."

"But to where, Christophe? You have a place picked out?"

"No. But the men will grow restless if we stay here. They know the soldiers will come now because of what happened."

"They have to find us first."

"Maybe that is hard to do," Christophe said, "if we keep moving."

"You become a moving target, Christophe. Here, there's one way in. They have to come one way, uphill, and much of it is in the open. *We* have cover. It's like Gettysburg, actually."

"I don't know Gettysburg, Donovan."

"The American Civil War. A huge battle. The south soldiers attacked the north soldiers, but it was open ground and uphill. They got slaughtered. It was pretty brave, though."

"How many men fighting at Gettysburg?" Christophe said.

"Thousands. I think I read more than twelve thousand made that charge. But thousands were killed, too."

"How many soldiers will come here?"

"I don't know. Not twelve thousand. And maybe they don't know where to find us. And Gilles—he'll know what to do."

"*If* he comes back, Donovan."

"How long will you wait tomorrow, Christophe?"

"Until afternoon. Then we must move."

"You're certain?"

"No."

"Have some rum, Christophe."

"I will, thank you."

Donovan did not sleep well and woke up with the dawn. He had dreamed of the road and the shooting and the man he had killed and after he had a drink from his canteen, he took a sip of what was left from the rum bottle. He looked for his carbine and saw it still leaning against the trunk of a tree. He realized it was becoming instinctual to know where his weapon was. He also realized it was not so wise to lean it against a tree. He knew Gilles would have lectured him on that.

Jean-Paul brought him legim and avocado.

"Is there any more herring, Jean-Paul?"

"All gone. You want more legim?"

"No. I think we must conserve food now. Have you eaten, Jean-Paul?"

"Of course."

"Really?"

Jean-Paul looked away.

"I will now."

"Be sure that you do – please," Donovan said.

"You do not need to say please when it is an order," Jean-Paul said.

Donovan wanted to tell him that it was not an order because he was not a soldier, but he didn't think Jean-Paul would accept that.

"There is food left for you, Jean-Paul?"

"Yes, we have food. I will go eat."

"Thanks, my friend."

Donovan picked up his carbine and decided to walk

down the slope to see how the sentries were doing. At the first station, they were still sleeping. He woke them gently and they looked embarrassed.

"What would Christophe say?"

"We have not seen Christophe since yesterday," one of them said.

"You'll see him today," Donovan said. "One of you should go to camp and bring back food."

They both smiled, and one of them jumped up and sprinted toward camp.

"I'm going farther down to the next station. Please don't shoot me when I come back."

Donovan added a smile, and the man smiled, too.

"A joke," the man said.

"Yes. Much of all this is a joke."

At the next station, Donovan was pleasantly surprised to see the men were all up and alert. But they were hungry, too, and he sent one up the slope for food.

"Tell your comrade at the next station not to shoot you by mistake," Donovan called after the man, and the other men all laughed.

"Thank you, Father," one of the men said.

"Don't call me Father. I'll send Christophe later to check on you."

"You will have to *find* Christophe first," one of the men said, and the others laughed.

They really were good men, Donovan believed, despite the utter lack of discipline, and he wished he had some rum to give them. After checking to see if they still had water, he walked back to camp, sat under his tree, and daydreamed for a bit. It was all he could think of to do, all there really was to do for now. This time, he placed his carbine in the security of a crook of a tree trunk facing away from himself and camp.

Donovan had not seen Christophe since the night before. It was early afternoon, and the deadline to move the camp was creeping closer. Where had Christophe gone? Was he cowardly enough to desert? He asked Jean-Paul, who also had not seen him, and Donovan began to worry. When Christophe finally did appear, Donovan learned he had merely been scouting a few miles from the camp for somewhere to move the men. He felt bad that he had doubted Christophe, who was mostly just not a soldier instead of a coward. Christophe nodded when he returned and then settled under a tree for a short nap.

Donovan shouldered his carbine and stood there a moment, surveying the men in camp. Some napped while others checked weapons and even cleaned them – a good sign that things had not yet completely fallen apart. He located Jean-Paul and made sure the boy had eaten something. Then he walked down to the first sentry post. One of the men was asleep but the other was alert and that was acceptable.

"Jean-Paul is bringing you food," he said to the man. "Do you have water?"

"Plenty of water," the man said, holding up his canteen and grinning.

If there was to be a fight, Donovan thought, these men would fight well enough. They had at Bauzain. The question was, how well would *he* fight? He already had, he reminded himself. That threshold had been crossed and he had survived it.

But Donovan also began to wonder whether it made sense to have this first sentry post since there was a second one much further down the slope. The second post would be the first to know if something was coming and then they would have to pull back to camp and take the men from the next post with them. The first post, he realized, had no real function anymore. It would have made more sense to move the first post's sentries down to the second one and fortify it some more. He was learning and might yet make a proper soldier.

"Once you two eat," he told the man, "you can go down to the next post."

"Are we leaving this camp soon, Father?"

"I don't know." Donovan decided not to make a big deal over being called Father. "Do you need to hear this from Christophe?"

The man shook his head and grinned again.

"I do not need to hear too much from Christophe, Father."

Donovan walked down to the second post and was very happy to see Gilles there talking with the men.

"I am told it was your idea to push sentries down here," Gilles said. "Good thinking, my friend."

Donovan offered a hand and smiled broadly as they shook.

"Can't tell you how glad I am to see you, Gilles. Christophe wants to move the camp. I tried to talk him out of it, but he insisted."

"So I am told," Gilles said. "I'll attend to that."

"How's Michel?"

"Safe," Gilles said. "He will recover. But not for a while."

Donovan felt weight slip off his shoulders.

"I prayed for him."

"Even though you are not a priest?"

"Even though I'm not a priest. But a man can still pray."

Gilles nodded, glanced at the four sentries, and frowned. He looked again at Donovan without saying anything. Donovan noticed the frown, wondered what it meant, and knew it was likely not good, and something Gilles preferred to keep between the two of them for the time being.

"Be alert," Gilles said to the sentries. "Now is not the time to nap. Do you understand me?"

"Yes," one of the four sentries said.

"No falling asleep," Gilles said. "Not now."

"We are awake," the man said. "I can assure you."

"I will come back very soon to check things here," Gilles said. "Very soon. After I see Christophe."

All four sentries nodded gravely and clutched their AKs firmly, and Donovan thought it was all pretty ominous and a touch surreal, too. He waited as patiently as he could as they walked up the slope and out of earshot of the sentries.

"What's wrong, Gilles? It's the soldiers, isn't it? They're coming?"

"They were always going to be coming – eventually. But now, we have stirred a nest. What is that saying?"

"You must mean 'stirred up a hornet's nest,' I guess."

"Yes. Hornets." Gilles stopped and looked at him. "There have been some developments, my friend."

"Have the soldiers decided to give us medals and throw us a feast?"

Donovan smiled, and Gilles couldn't help but smile, too.

"It would be nice to think so," Gilles said. "And I am happy you still have your sense of humor. But we have been betrayed instead. Someone told the soldiers where to look for us."

"Damn. Not good."

"There is more."

"It gets worse?"

"Have you ever heard of these things getting better?"

Donovan shrugged.

"I guess I was hoping for some red snapper and Prestige down on the beach."

"Not in Les Cayes, Donovan. Not ever again in Les Cayes. The soldier who got away yesterday – he recognized you and I. So, if you ever decide to be a priest again, I suggest *not* in Les Cayes."

"Good God."

"Yes," Gilles said. "A good God would be very useful about now."

"Well, this will certainly vindicate Christophe."

"It does not," Gilles said. "You were right to advocate staying here, based on what you knew at the time. This is a good position. But now it has been compromised. Christophe could not know that, and his decision was based more on panic than strategy and information. But nonetheless – yes, now we must move."

"When?"

"As soon as we can. Right away is not too soon. Now we go find Christophe and make him a hero."

* * *

Donovan and Gilles sat under a tree and watched as the rebels slowly collected their weapons and possessions. They moved slowly. Christophe strolled among them, urging them to hurry.

"Christophe is finally embracing command," Donovan said. "Better late than never, I suppose."

"There is precious little commanding left," Gilles said.

"What am I missing here?"

"This is just between us – for now."

"Why don't I like the sound of this?"

"I have been recalled," Gilles said without emotion.

Donovan stared at him a moment, not quite understanding.

"Recalled? What does that mean?"

"I have been summoned to America."

"By the CIA?"

"Well, not by the Boys Scouts. Yes, I am to report to Langley."

Donovan watched the men packing.

"And what about these folks? And where do *I* go now, if you don't mind me asking?

"You go with me," Gilles said. "The rebels cease to be rebels for now and go home, to their towns and villages and farms – wherever they came from, they go back to.

"They just don't know that yet."

"I will tell them once they are on their feet and actually ready to move. We avoid more delays that way. And they are less likely to sit and debate it."

"Does Christophe know?"

"No. But Christophe will be happy to go home. They all will. Without a true leader, for now, it is safer that they stop being soldiers and pretend to just be villagers."

"And I go with you?"

"You do. I just said so."

"Where?"

"Cuba."

"Cuba? You do know that Cuba is run by a guy named Fidel, right?"

"We will go to Guantanamo. Fidel does not run Guantanamo."

"And how do we *get* to Guantanamo?"

"It is not so far, really. Just across the strait from Jeremie, and Jeremie is not so far from here."

"Are we swimming to Cuba?"

"Fishing boat," Gilles said. "It is already arranged. Or do you prefer to stay behind – go back to Les Cayes, perhaps?"

"I guess I've seen enough of Les Cayes. How do we get to Jeremie?"

"We walk, my friend."

"How many miles is it?"

"Do not think in terms of how far it is," Gilles said. "Think of it as an opportunity – an opportunity to avoid being shot by Baby Doc's soldiers."

"I'm warming up to a good hike, I guess. But do we really have to walk it?"

"It is safer that way. We must stay off the roads. They are looking for us."

"What are our chances?"

"Good – if we can get out of here soon," Gilles said. "We know where we are going, and the soldiers do not."

"I could drink to that."

Gilles pulled a bottle of Rhum Barbancourt from his pack.

"One for the road, Donovan."

"Well, if we're going to Cuba, better make it two."

Donovan took a long pull of rum. It caught fire in his stomach and warmed him. For just the briefest moment, he forgot about the man he killed.

Chapter Sixteen

Gilles and Donovan waited to approach Christophe until after the rebels, perhaps eighty men, had begun to fall into a sloppy column. Christophe blinked rapidly a few times as Gilles told him it was time to disband and go home. Christophe looked down at the ground and shuffled his feet.

"It is over, Gilles? Truly?"

"My friend, it is—suspended. For now, anyway. But the fight continues."

"It does?"

"Just not here, not now."

Donovan wanted to say something but couldn't think of what to say. He looked at the men forming a column.

"And later?" Christophe said. "What about Baby Doc? What about the soldiers in Les Cayes?"

Gilles shook his head.

"The soldiers are coming, Christophe. They come now. And there are too many. Port-au-Prince sent reinforcements."

"And Baby Doc?"

"Protests will continue elsewhere," Gilles said. "Just not

here."

"The CIA has given up?" Christophe said. "America has given up?"

"No," Gilles said. "But I have been called to America to report on what is happening."

"You will come back?"

"It would not surprise me, Christophe."

"Soon?"

"That also would not surprise me," Gilles said.

Christophe looked at Donovan.

"What will *you* do, Donovan?"

"I have to go with Gilles. I can't stay here."

"No," Christophe said, looking sad. "I suppose you cannot."

Gilles offered a hand, and Christophe looked at it for a moment before accepting.

"Now you must tell your men," Gilles said. "Now you must be a leader again and send them home. Tell them to hide their weapons and wait."

"Wait for what?"

"For Michel," Gilles said. "Tell them to wait until Michel is back. Tell them I go to America, and I will tell people there that this must not end."

"You can convince them, Gilles?" Christophe said.

"I will do my best, yes."

"Bless you, Gilles. I will do as you ask."

"Stay strong, Christophe. It is not yet over."

"I will hope to believe that," Christophe said.

Christophe and Donovan shook hands, and Christophe walked to the head of the rebel column with his head down.

"Get your pack, Donovan," Gilles said. "We must leave

now. We should have left already."

The rebel column moved out toward the east, and Gilles and Donovan headed north, but they stopped after a few yards and watched the last of the rebels disappear into the jungle before setting off again.

"How far, Gilles? The truth this time."

"Several days. We hike parallel to the road to Roseaux. From Roseaux, I think we can get a ride to Jeremie. Then Cuba."

"Sounds simple enough. But all the best plans start off simply enough."

"There is nothing simple in Haiti these days."

* * *

They walked past sundown until there was a full moon and made camp in a grove of trees shielded from the road to Roseaux. Gilles had brought more dried herring and several containers of rice and beans.

"We have to make the food last," Gilles said. "At Roseaux, we can eat a proper meal."

"Some hot tchaka and legim would sound good about now."

"Pretend the herring is red snapper or yellowtail."

"And the rice and beans?"

"Pretend they are caviar," Gilles said.

"Should I also pretend there's a hot shower and silk sheets?"

"It might rain tomorrow, Donovan – that will be your shower."

"The shower will be cold."

"We cannot have everything. But the scenery is good, no?"

"Excellent scenery, Gilles."

After they ate, Gilles produced the bottle of Rhum Barbancourt.

"Just a little rum, and water afterward. We don't want to dehydrate."

The rum exploded in Donovan's stomach, and he felt a pleasant glow. He knew he would sleep soon. They had walked far. His legs ached.

"When do we get there, Gilles?"

"On the morning after tomorrow. We have food enough for tomorrow. But breakfast after that must be in Roseaux."

"We can't just walk into Roseaux carrying an AK-47 and a carbine."

"True. We must leave them outside of the town." Gilles reached into his pack and retrieved the .32 and extra clip. "Here, you will need this again when we reach Roseaux."

"Let's hope not."

Donovan checked the safety and then slipped the gun into his pack. He leaned back against a tree trunk and looked up at the moon through a gap in the treetops.

"Do you know how far we walked today, Gilles?"

"I could speculate, in kilometers. Or would you prefer miles?"

"Well, miles would sound shorter," Donovan said. "And it would sound American since that's where we're going."

"Do you really want to know an exact distance?"

"No. Not really. It doesn't matter. It would just be a number."

"What *does* matter, Donovan?"

"I'm not sure anymore. Surviving, I guess. But for what?"

"Never worry about what you are surviving for – until you have actually survived it."

"They teach you that at CIA school?"

"My mother taught me that. She is Haitian, after all."

"Good advice."

"What did *your* mother teach you?" Gilles said.

Donovan thought a moment, but nothing came to him.

"My mother encouraged me to become a priest."

"Is that why you almost did?"

"Maybe. I wanted to please her. That's true enough. But now I see you have to please yourself if you're going to be good enough to please others."

"Profound," Gilles said. "But what does it mean?"

"It means sometimes you have to walk away from home before you can find it."

"You did not learn that in priest school."

"No. I learned that in Haiti."

* * *

The next morning, they ate rice and beans for breakfast to save the dried herring for lunch and dinner. As Gilles predicted, it rained and soaked them, but they kept walking with only short breaks until lunch of dried herring and several bananas Donovan had in his pack. Just before dark, they reached a bend in the Riviere Roseaux and filled their canteens.

"We are close now," Gilles said. "Roseaux is ahead."

"How far?"

"In miles—perhaps three or four."

"Don't tell me in kilometers," Donovan said, smiling. Gilles smiled, too.

"We're practically there. Numbers do not matter."

"Do we go on in?"

"No. It will be dark very soon. We wait for the morning, when we can see where we are going in the town. We can stay here by the river."

"Okay," Donovan said, slipping off his pack. "So, what shall we have for dinner?"

"Would dried herring meet your approval?"

"Miraculous. I haven't had dried herring since – lunch."

"But no herring for breakfast. I promise. We will get something decent in Roseaux."

"Is it safe there?"

"If we don't linger."

"How far is Jeremie from Roseaux?"

"Perhaps five miles. Do you want to know in kilometers?"

"God, no."

"In Roseaux," Gilles said, "we can look for a vehicle going to Jeremie."

"We can walk it if we have to. We just need food."

"That is the spirit, Donovan."

When it was dark and they had finished the last of the herring, they each had a drink of rum.

"The Boy Scouts were never like this," Donovan said. "Machine guns and rum."

"We dump our rifles first thing in the morning," Gilles said. "But we keep the rum."

"Medicinal."

* * *

They woke up very early the next morning and approached Roseaux from just off the road from Les Cayes and were careful not to be seen from the road.

"Roseaux is a poor, small town," Gilles said. "And perhaps just far enough from Port-au-Prince for us to slip in and out quickly, though you are too tall, Donovan. Can you hunch over some as you walk?"

"Seriously?"

"I kid. You will yet figure that out."

A vehicle came from the south, and they looked through the trees at the road in time to see a government truck with a few soldiers standing up in the bed and carrying AK-47s.

"Well, so much for going unnoticed," Donovan said.

"They have come up from Les Cayes," Gilles said as he watched the truck go by into Roseaux.

"Looking for us?"

"They cannot know we are here. And it is only a handful of soldiers. Most likely, it is routine. But it changes our plan."

"We walk to Jeremie."

"Yes. But first, I will go into Roseaux and get food."

"It's too dangerous, Gilles."

"I am Haitian, remember? I can mingle unnoticed."

"Okay. But be quick. I don't want to have to shoot my way in and rescue you."

"That would be foolish, Donovan, but dramatic."

"But you would do it for *me*, right?"

Gilles squeezed Jeremy's shoulder.

"You keep thinking that, my friend. It is a lovely notion."

"That's what I thought."

Gilles handed his AK to Donovan and retrieved his 9 mm pistol from his pack. Donovan retrieved the .32 from his pack and offered it to Gilles.

"Here. Now you're the one who may need this. Two pistols are better than one."

Gilles slipped it into a back pocket.

"I do not disagree."

"Seriously," Donovan said. "If something happens to you, what do I do?"

"Nothing is going to happen. But if it does, go up the coast to Jeremie." He wrote a name on a scrap of paper the herring had been wrapped in and gave it to him. "Look for this man, a fisherman. He is our ride to Cuba. It is arranged. One passenger, or two – all the same to the fisherman."

"You take care of yourself in there, Gilles."

"Always."

Chapter Seventeen

Gilles was gone several hours and, to pass the time, Donovan daydreamed about hiking along Lake Michigan. It was quite pleasant, and he could visualize everything he knew so well from growing up there, the dunes, the gulls, the lapping waves. He could almost feel the wet sand under his feet and feel the cooling breeze off the blue mass of the lake.

He might have drifted into a nap at that point, but abruptly, he heard a vehicle coming and clutched the AK. He poked its snout through an opening in the trees toward the road. It was the government truck coming out of Roseaux, but no soldiers stood in its bed this time. The truck stopped beside the road, in front of the grove of trees sheltering him, and he pulled back the AK's bolt and aimed at the truck. Sweat dripped off his forehead, and his hands were moist and clammy; he needed a better grip on the AK.

A man got out of the driver's side and, when he walked around to the other side, Donovan saw it was Gilles. He lowered the AK and jumped up as Gilles waved him out of the grove.

"Get in, Donovan. Hurry!"

Donovan ran to the truck and jumped in as Gilles climbed back in, started it up, and made a U-turn on the road back toward Roseaux.

"I know there's a great story behind this," Donovan said. "I'm listening."

Gilles grinned.

"I found a ride. How do you like it?"

"Baby Doc's personal jet wasn't available, Gilles?"

"Sadly, I would have passed on the jet. I do not know how to fly."

"I don't even want to ask what happened to the soldiers, but – what the hell happened to the soldiers, Gilles?"

They were passing through Roseaux, and Gilles gunned it. Several Haitian girls were standing by the road ahead.

"Wave, Donovan, so they think we are soldiers. Hold up your AK."

Jeremy held up his AK and Gilles waved, and the girls waved back and smiled.

"This is insane," Donovan said, still smiling and waving.

"You would rather walk? I can let you out. Just tell me where."

He took his foot off the gas, and the truck began to slow.

"For God's sake, keep going—and tell me what happened to the soldiers."

"Nothing happened to them."

"Then where are they? How'd you get this truck?"

"Well, as it turns out, they were a little drunk," Gilles said. "And they became more drunk and fell asleep on the beach. You know our good Haitian rum. Anyway, they were kind enough to leave the keys in their truck, and I took that as permission to borrow it for a time."

"They'll kill us, Gilles."

"How? Soon, they will be five miles behind us, and they are passed out on a beach without a vehicle. And we are going to Cuba."

Donovan smirked.

"That's some mighty good thinking."

"I thought you might appreciate it."

"Did you get us any food?"

"I am afraid not. But we can eat in Jeremie. We will be there very soon."

* * *

Gilles turned off Rue La Source Dommage in Jeremie and parked the truck in a thick grove of trees not far beyond the harbor where it wouldn't be immediately spotted. Gilles returned the .32 to Donovan. They hiked back to the harbor, and Gilles chatted in French with several Haitian men while Donovan looked out over the harbor into the Caribbean. Cuba was out there somewhere. Guantanamo. The American base. Safety. No more Baby Doc and his soldiers. How far it was to Cuba, and the specific direction, he did not yet know.

"Good news," Gilles said. "There are no soldiers here in Jeremie."

"Great—just the ones asleep on the beach a few miles from here."

"They may as well be one hundred miles from here."

"What about this boat captain of yours, Gilles? I hope he's a hell of a lot closer than a hundred miles."

"The captain is only about one hundred *yards* from here," Gilles said. "That is his boat, down there in the last slip."

"How do you know?"

"I asked those men," Gilles said. "One of them crews the boat sometimes."

"No crafty CIA stuff—you just asked for directions?"

"Sometimes that is the best way."

"What would James Bond say to that?"

"James Bond would order a martini – shaken and not stirred," Gilles said.

"That sounds good about now."

"First, I find the captain."

Gilles walked toward the boat.

"What should I do?"

"Try not to look so tall. I will be back in a few minutes."

"I'll be right here – slouching, I guess."

But Donovan felt self-consciously tall and American and wished he could hide somewhere, but there really was nowhere to go, so he sat on a bench and tried to ignore his hunger as he watched white gulls circle and land until Gilles returned.

"Ready to go to Cuba, Donovan?"

"As ready as I'll ever be. What about our captain?"

"The boat is fueled. We leave right away."

"He knows the way?"

"Cuba is a big island, Donovan. He assured me he can find it."

"Is there time to get something to eat?"

"No," Gilles said. "But the captain says he will feed us. And it keeps us out of the village and prying eyes."

"What's on the menu?"

"Beans and rice. And dried fish."

"But not dried herring. Please, tell me it's not dried herring."

"Yes—I believe that it is. Do you suppose he knew it is your favorite, Donovan?"

* * *

Donovan learned that the boat captain's name was – captain.

"No names," the captain said. "Better for everyone."

"What will you call me, then?" Donovan said.

"Passenger number two."

"Number two? Why can't I be number one?"

The captain pointed at Gilles.

"He paid. He is passenger number one."

Gilles laughed.

"Next time, you can handle the money, number two."

"Next time."

The captain was fiftyish and had deep lines etched in his dark face from years at sea. He called to Gilles to cast off the stern line.

"And you, get the bow line," the captain said to Donovan.

"Do you mean passenger one or passenger two?" Donovan said.

The captain turned to Gilles.

"Are you sure he is with you?"

"He means well," Gilles said, but he smiled.

"I'll just go get the bow line," Donovan said. "That's the front of the boat, you know."

The captain shook his head and then turned the engines over. They belched and then roared to life. After Donovan had slipped the bow line and jumped aboard, the captain backed her out of the slip into the harbor toward the open sea. As they left the harbor, Gilles looked ahead, but Donovan stood on the stern, looking back as the harbor and shoreline diminished. He studied the green mountains behind the town. Mist had begun to settle on them. Gilles went to the stern.

"Cuba is the other way, Donovan. What are you looking at?"

"The end of Haiti."

* * *

The stoic captain steered into the Caribbean. Gilles brought bowls of beans and rice up from the galley and gave one first to the captain, who nodded politely and ate while he steered, and then to Donovan, who sat near the stern watching porpoises racing alongside the boat.

"Thanks," Donovan said. "But I'll pass on the herring. And this is my last bowl of beans and rice for some time to come."

"Me, too, Donovan. Me, too."

They ate quietly, the protective hum of the engines behind them. Donovan glanced over his shoulder once as he ate and could still see Haiti, but it was faint and becoming more like a mirage than a real shoreline.

"How far is it – to Guantanamo?" Donovan said after he sat down his bowl.

"More than one hundred miles, I believe."

"When will we get there?"

"Late tonight. Or perhaps very early in the morning. The captain will decide that. His boat, his fuel, his speed."

"Captain captain," Donovan said quietly, and Gilles grinned too. "Will there be a marching band waiting for us, Gilles?"

"I forgot to arrange it – forgive me. Would you settle for

random seashells on the beach?"

"Sure. Why not."

Donovan looked out again at the playful porpoises. Then he looked back at Gilles and frowned.

"What do you mean by random seashells on the beach?"

"We'll be swimming from the boat to the beach. Oh, did I forget to mention that?"

"Well – yeah, you did."

"An oversight."

"Swimming to shore," Donovan said flatly. "What's wrong with pulling alongside a dock and stepping off like civilized folks?"

"Guantanamo is an American base, a military base. We are on a foreign ship. See the dilemma?"

"But you're CIA, Gilles."

"We are not flying a CIA flag."

"Don't you guys have those?"

"I believe there are some at Langley."

"So – just how far will we have to swim?"

"You *can* swim, right, Donovan?"

"Yes, I can. But what if I couldn't?"

"I would buy one of the captain's lifejackets and tow you in."

"You have an answer for everything."

"I have brought you this far, correct?"

Donovan nodded.

"Yeah, you did. And I appreciate it. And I can use a bath, so we'll swim it, I guess."

"If it helps," Gilles said," I believe the captain will slow down as we jump overboard."

"Very kind of him. Did you have to pay extra for that?"

"Not at all. He was quite good about that."

"He's a man of few words, but many virtues – is that it?"

"Something like that," Gilles said. "Mostly he is a man who has a price."

A minute later, Donovan said, "And how far will we have to swim?"

"Certainly not as far as we will have to walk once we make land. Look at it that way."

"Is it that far from the beach to the base?"

"Well, it is where *we* will be landing."

"We're not landing at the base?"

"A little south of there."

"How far south?"

"Ten miles, I believe," Gilles said.

"What?"

"Notice I did not say it in kilometers."

"Very considerate."

"My mother taught me that."

"Why don't we just land near the base?"

"The captain cannot get that close—we could be shot at if he did. So, we steer a bit south of the base."

"And you know the way to the base – without getting us shot once we're there?"

"No."

"How reassuring."

"But someone will meet us who does. He knows we are coming."

"Is it Fidel Castro, Gilles?"

"Good, Donovan. You still have not lost your sense of humor. I confess that I thought you would."

"Who is this person meeting us?"

"Someone from the CIA. I know him."

"Couldn't he just pick us up in a car?"

"We don't want to draw attention to ourselves. We will be in Cuba rather illegally. So, we walk it and stay away from roads – and Fidel Castro."

"I see. A lot of that going around. So – is there any rum left?"

"In my pack. I will go get it."

The rum helped Donovan slip into a nap. When he woke up, it was night, and the captain was sitting across from him eating beans and rice as Gilles steered.

"Good evening, passenger number two," the captain said. "How was your nap?"

"I dreamt I was on a boat, and nobody had names – go figure."

"Then you might as well have stayed awake," the captain said.

"Good to know. You trust passenger number one to steer?"

"If he stays on our heading, we will be fine."

"I don't doubt it. He's a man of many talents."

"Is it true you are a priest?" the captain said abruptly.

"I thought you didn't want to know anything about your passengers. That it's just business."

"I ask this not from business, but for my own curiosity," the captain said. "Priests, nuns, or devils – all the same as cargo as long as they behave."

"Had many devils aboard?"

"You might be surprised."

"Not anymore. Once, I could be surprised."

"As a priest?"

"I'm not a priest."

"I see," the captain said as he rubbed his chin.

That seemed to satisfy the captain's limited curiosity, and

he eased back to take a short nap.

Donovan went forward to Gilles.

"Just so you know, Gilles – our captain is asleep, we're in the middle of the Caribbean in the middle of the night, and Fidel Castro is waiting for us."

"Right out of a novel, is it not?"

"Let's just make sure it has a happy ending."

"No one can predict the future."

"Very reassuring."

"Here," Gilles said, pointing at the compass on the dashboard just above the steering wheel. "This is our heading – take over for a minute while I go below to pee."

Donovan grabbed the wheel and checked the compass as Gilles disappeared down the stairs to the galley. He wondered what the captain would do if he nudged the throttle forward a little, but thought better of the idea. The boat handled well, and the vibrations from the engines pulsated along the hull and up into the steering wheel and into his hands. It was a pleasant experience. He liked having something to do. When Gilles came back, he asked to steer a while longer, and Gilles slid into the other seat across from him.

"Joining the Navy, Donovan?"

"I thought I worked for the CIA."

"Technically, you do not work for us. You are not being paid."

"But I'm earning much experience, Gilles."

"Then you are a rich man."

"Yet I dress and smell like a dirty refugee."

"Not much longer," Gilles said. "How is our heading?"

"Dead on."

"Do not say dead," Gilles said. "Bad luck."

"I get your point. Our heading is – accurate."
"Or steady. Our heading could be said to be steady."
"I feel like an admiral already, Gilles."
"Admirals do not steer."
"I'm a hands-on admiral."
"Commendable, Donovan. You are a man of the people."
"What if I let our heading drift to the left a bit, Gilles. Would we miss Cuba?"
"Yes. And hit Jamaica."
"Jamaica might be fun."
"Without doubt, Donovan. All those drinks with umbrellas in them. But the CIA directed me to Guantanamo, and so we go to Guantanamo."

After a minute, Donovan said, "What does all this add up to, Gilles?"

"Cuba. No more Haiti. A flight to Miami. A margarita on Miami Beach."

"No, I mean the time in Haiti. The rebels. Les Cayes. Michel, Christophe, and Jean-Paul. What does all that add up to?"

"Now is not the time to know that, my friend. Later, with perspective."

"Can you be just a bit more philosophical, Gilles?"

"But it is true. We are too close to events now to understand them fully. Now we are just carried along by them. Understanding comes much later."

Donovan pretended to check their heading again.

"And will I get perspective on killing a man, Gilles?"

"Yes. You will. You did the right thing. It had to be done."

"I know. But that doesn't make it go away."

"It will live with you forever. But if it did not, you would not be much of a man."

Donovan thought for a moment.

"Do you remember Christophe's last words? He said, 'I shall hope to believe that.'"

"I heard them, yes."

Donovan replayed the shooting scene in his head but was able to stop it after a moment and focus on the humming engines and the vibrations radiating all the way to his hands on the wheel.

"What will happen in Haiti now, Gilles?"

"I cannot know that."

"Speculate – guess, for God's sake."

"I believe Baby Doc must eventually go. Maybe soon, maybe not so soon."

"And that will make it all worthwhile?"

"Doing our best while we were there makes it all worthwhile."

"Did we do our best?"

"We did as much as we could."

"You're an idealist, Gilles."

"Is that so bad?"

"No. It's one of the very few things worth being, I suspect."

"And you, Donovan? What are you?"

"I'm passenger number two – remember?"

"I think soon you will come out from under the humor," Gilles said, "and know surely who you are."

"Think so? Well, we'll see."

Donovan turned the wheel back to Gilles.

"You should eat something again, Donovan. Soon, we will have much to do. You will need your strength."

Donovan went down to the galley and reluctantly munched dried herring and then napped again.

* * *

Gilles shook him awake.

"It is almost time. We must go."

Donovan had dreamt of Lake Michigan again. In his dream, he had spoken with a blue heron. He had no idea why but decided not to question it. He sat up for a moment and then they went up on deck. It was still dark, and the boat's engines idled. The captain was at the wheel.

"What time is it?" Donovan said. He was not yet fully awake, his eyes still adjusting to the darkness.

"Very early morning," Gilles said. "Do you need a shot of rum to wake up?"

"Yes."

They both sipped rum, and Gilles gave the bottle to the captain, who also sipped.

"Keep the bottle, captain, for the trip home."

"I think you need it more than me," he said, handing it back.

"It is dead weight in the water," Gilles said.

The captain said something in French, and Gilles replied in French. Gilles smiled and patted the captain's shoulder.

"He has given us an inflatable raft, Donovan. We can land in dry clothes."

"To show I am a good son of Haiti," the captain said. "And a good Catholic after all."

"Bless you," Donovan said, feeling odd but meaning it.

Gilles held the wheel, and the captain retrieved the raft from below and inflated it, and they eased it over the side. The sea was calm and there was not much moon. Donovan was finally able to make out the Cuban shore. Gilles shook hands with the captain as Donovan slid over the side into the raft.

"Thank you, captain," Donovan said.

"Tell that bastard Castro to kiss my ass," the captain said.

"If I see him, I'll be sure to do it."

Gilles climbed in, and they paddled toward shore.

Chapter Eighteen

Donovan sipped a margarita at a table by the pool of a sumptuous hotel on Miami Beach. He glanced at young women in bikinis, their sleek bodies coated in oils, and from the soft breeze tickling his forehead, he caught the scent of coconut. When the waiter asked for his order, he said, "Nothing with rum in it."

He had slept for ten hours, showered and shaved, and slipped on new, clean clothes – a navy polo and khaki slacks – before he ate a late breakfast of scrambled eggs, bacon, sausage, hash browns, orange juice, and wheat toast. No beans. No rice. No dried herring. No sleeping on the ground.

No Haiti.

Just American soil. Well—sand.

Just American chow.

He was on his second margarita when Gilles showed up. They had flown together from Guantanamo the day before, courtesy of the CIA. Gilles wore a white linen suit without a tie, a white shirt with an open collar underneath his jacket, and he carried a folded *Miami Herald*. He had shaved and gotten a good haircut, a bit of oil in his hair to make it lay down nicely, and Donovan thought he looked a bit like a gigolo prowling for a rich, older woman.

"Well, it is noon somewhere in the world," Gilles said, noting the half-full margarita in Donovan's hand, and he, too glanced at the bikini-clad women.

"It's almost noon *here*, Gilles. Close enough."

"Indeed."

Gilles declined a drink when the waiter came by.

"So, what's next for you, Gilles? Another revolution, far off in a strange land?"

"Langley. I have a flight this afternoon."

"To talk about Haiti."

"It would not surprise me if it came up."

"You have to do right by them, Gilles. You have to do right by Michel, Jean-Paul, and Christophe. You know that, right?"

"It is never far from my thoughts."

The waiter asked Donovan if he wanted another drink, but he declined.

"Two's enough," he said after the waiter left. "I may try to sober up a little."

"No rum, I see, Donovan."

"No more rum for a lifetime, maybe."

Gilles nodded.

"What is next for you, my friend? Do you have any money?"

"Yes. I was able to get some from my bank."

"Are you rich, Donovan?"

"God, no. But I have some savings."

"And now you go back to Michigan and your big, grand lake?"

"In the morning, by train."

"I could arrange something for you by air. You have some money in the bank, so to say, with the CIA."

Donovan chuckled and glanced again at the oiled bodies barely covered by bikinis.

"Never in my life did I expect to hear that the CIA owed me a favor. Forgive me if I confess that it's surreal."

"You did not get paid for Haiti," Gilles said. "Probably you should have. But they would be happy to fly you home."

"Thanks, but no. I always like a train ride. I want to see a little of America on the way. I want to decompress more before going home."

"It will be very different from Haiti."

"I'm counting on that."

"So, home, and home cooking and all that," Gilles said.

"My mom likes to make beans and rice," Donovan said abruptly, laughing, and Gilles laughed too.

"What else can she make?"

"She also makes a wicked meatloaf."

"I suggest the meatloaf."

"And no dried herring."

Several children splashed in the pool. Their mothers chatted happily in chaise lounges in bathing suits and sunglasses. Tourists began to flock to tables for lunch.

"It's all very civilized here," Donovan said. "Everyone is – correct."

Gilles nodded and watched the children for a moment. "Very."

"Do you have children, Gilles? A wife? I guess I never asked."

"A son, Phillipe, in Paris. With his mother. He is ten."

"You will see them soon?"

"Yes. Very soon."

"That's good, Gilles. I will say a prayer for you and them."

"Most welcome, my friend. But you are not a priest – remember?"

"I can still pray. We can all pray. It never hurts to pray."

"No, it does not hurt. I agree."

"Did you ever pray in Haiti, Gilles?"

He looked away at the children splashing water.

"Well, I often hoped for the best."

"A holdout to the end. Is that right?"

"Perhaps. Will you stay in Michigan, Donovan?"

"I don't know."

"And why should you know? Certainly not today. You have just arrived. Take your time, my friend."

"All the time in the world, right?"

"We like to think so," Gilles said. "Have you considered writing about your time in Haiti?"

"You mean a book?"

"Yes, a book. You saw what it was like. People should know."

"What should they know, Gilles?"

"The truth. As you experienced it."

"And what's the truth?"

"Well, that is for you to decide when you write it."

After a moment, Donovan said, "Thanks for getting me home, Gilles. Truly."

He offered his hand across the table, and they shook vigorously.

"All part of the job, Donovan."

"I think not."

"Well, we shall say it is."

"Fair enough, Gilles."

Gilles glanced at the children in the pool again and then got up.

"I must go now. I would rather sit here by the pool and drink with you. That would be preferable. But I have obligations. "

"I've heard of those."

"Be well, Donovan."

"Will I ever see you again, Gilles?"

"It would not surprise me."

"I'd like that, Gilles."

"As would I, old friend."

"You take good care of yourself."

"Always. If I do not, who will?"

Gilles smiled, patted Donovan's shoulder, and walked away. Donovan turned in his chair and watched him disappear inside the hotel, and then went back to watching oiled bodies in bikinis.

Chapter Nineteen

The train to Michigan was slow but pleasant, and he slept surprisingly well overnight in the seat. It was better than the damp ground in Haiti. Donovan was content to watch the landscape ease past his window and absorb the changes from tropical to Midwest. In the club car, he ate a hamburger with French fries covered in ketchup. It was a microwaved burger, but it tasted heavenly to him.

His parents didn't know he was coming, of course, and his last letter from Haiti was more than a month old. Naturally, it had been an upbeat letter, designed to reassure them he was doing just fine and helping people and preserving Catholicism. The ancient empire. But he never called it that in letters to them. He didn't mention rebels in the hills or Baby Doc or the CIA or a boat ride to Cuba. Or the fact he had killed a man. That little detail would have to remain private for the time being. Maybe forever.

It would all be a lot for his parents to absorb. His mother would, of course, be disappointed. But Catholicism would have to preserve itself with one less priest. He knew it would do just fine without him because he'd never really been destined to become a priest, only to dance around the edges of faith, more a voyeur than anything else. He was not an empire builder. He was just a man. A man headed home to see what it still meant to him. It was easier to live as just a man. Simplicity was underrated.

Inevitably, he thought again of the soldier he had killed. He never saw his face. Never saw his body. He knew that was probably a mercy. His death was a concept more than a visual in some ways – but real enough. But not seeing the body – very fortunate. That would make it much easier to make peace with it. Well, maybe it was too optimistic to envision peace. Perhaps just adjusting to the necessity of having had to do it would be enough. That was the practical way to look at it.

He said a brief prayer for the man, whoever he was. He was sorry fate had put them on a collision course. But Gilles was right: there are moments in life when you must kill or be killed. It was a choice that had nothing to do with morality or ideology.

The sun was just coming up when the train crossed into Michigan, and Donovan watched it rise. It had been several years since he had been home. But he had been much younger then than time could adequately measure. He was not a boy anymore. And he was not coming home from the theoretical purity of a seminary. He was coming back from a revolution, a war of sorts, from having been, even briefly – a soldier. A soldier who had killed. In the mirror in the train's lavatory, he saw a very tanned face and longish hair and lines in a still handsome face, but an older face, an experienced face. A man's face and not a boy's innocent face. The boy was a memory. He had vanished.

He was eager to see his parents, but he dreaded it as well. His mother would be disappointed he had not chosen the church, and he had no idea yet how to tell her, but he couldn't allow that to affect what he knew to be true about himself: he was not a man committed solely to a marriage with God. He was a man who believed in God. Or perhaps hopeful there *was* a God. That was a better way to put it. More accurate.

He was a man willing to go to church *sometimes* and celebrate the possibility of God, but he didn't believe he would become a churchgoer. He was not one of God's soldiers. There were many ways to serve God and one of them was to be a good man with a good woman. He would never agree with the church on celibacy. He would never agree with it on a lot of things. Blind obedience was just out of the question.

The world was too complicated for that.

* * *

Donovan stayed with his parents for the remainder of the summer and in early fall found a full-time job tutoring for the school district and substitute teaching. He taught history and discovered he liked teaching and working with students. And in time, he didn't think of Haiti every day.

At first, there had been a few nightmares about the soldier he had killed, but even they disappeared soon enough. Mrs. Caldwell down the street from his parents had several rooms above her garage, and he rented them. He had just enough income for food and rent and a little left over.

The apartment was spartan – a bed and shower in a tiny bedroom, a small refrigerator and stove in the other room. Not so much of a higher standard than he had in Haiti. Cleaner, though. He bought an old easy chair and table and two chairs at a yard sale. Mrs. Caldwell donated silverware, plates, and glasses. There was a window with a view of Mrs. Caldwell's back porch and a large sycamore tree. He had no TV or car and figured to do just fine without them. Simplicity appealed to him.

Throughout the fall and winter, Donovan walked to work and then home and sometimes stopped at the library to get books, a mix of novels and history. He read some Fitzgerald – *Tender is the Night*, and Hemingway's *Islands in the Stream* because it took place in the Caribbean, and he was curious to know how Hemingway would portray the region. It felt familiar.

Hemingway's scenes on the Caribbean made him remember the details of the night journey from Haiti to Cuba, and he laughed out loud as he recalled it all. When he wasn't in the mood for fiction, he also read quite a few histories of the Civil War, and those relaxed him the most and enabled him to fall asleep.

Sometimes, he stopped at The Bohemian Tavern on the way home and drank a beer or two at the bar, or sometimes while playing the pinball machine in a corner. At first, a few people who remembered him would ask if he was still a priest, but after he told them he wasn't, never had been, and declined to elaborate, they eventually stopped asking and just accepted him as part of the bar's landscape. Just another person, which pleased him. He sometimes had his dinner at The Bohemian – Italian beef with mayonnaise and peppers was his favorite – while reading a Detroit or Grand Rapids newspaper.

Sometimes, on the way home from work, he would have dinner at his parents' house – by pre-arranged invitation – to see how they were doing and to let them know he was doing well. He was pleasantly surprised to see that his mother had gotten over her initial disappointment at his leaving the church, and she was proud that he was teaching. She thought that it suited him well, and he didn't disagree.

Sometimes, she still asked him to go to Mass with her, but he would politely decline, explaining that he just wasn't ready for that yet. He wasn't actually sure when he might be ready. Maybe never. Thankfully, she didn't press him. His new maturity had bestowed some leverage, he figured. Or maybe she'd just finally thrown in the towel.

* * *

His life slowed to a crawl. It became routine. Even dull. He drank more. One night, he sat in The Bohemian Tavern nursing a beer, watching the TV behind the bar, when he heard the unexpected news: Baby Doc had left Haiti for exile in France. He heard the news anchor's words but could not quite believe it was true, that it had finally happened.

He asked the bartender to turn it up and he saw footage from Haiti, some of it old, of bodies lying in streets, and giddy freedom fighters emptying AK magazines into the air, but also interviews with Haitians jubilant that it was finally over and the evil Baby Doc, as Gilles had predicted, had been made to go.

He wondered if Michel was still alive. What about Jean-Paul and good old, indecisive Christophe? And beautiful Emmanuella? She would have to cozy up to whatever it was that took over after Baby Doc, but he knew she'd do just fine. She was built for shifting allegiances. So were her parents. It would simply be business as usual for the Calezar clan. One of his lessons learned.

"Well," the bartender said after the news was over.

"What do you make of all that shit?"

But when the bartender turned back to Donovan, he'd already left. He walked home, flurries coming down hard, and he could not sleep until very late, his thoughts about Haiti a jumble of emotions. He wasn't sure how he felt or how he was supposed to feel. He believed he should feel more. Maybe that came later. It was a shock, but it all seemed far away now, too, like the distant craters on the moon. It was like a movie he'd seen a long time ago, and he couldn't quite remember the details accurately. Jumbled images of Haiti skyrocketed across his mind like it was the Fourth of July for distant memories.

Just before he finally fell asleep, with the help of a tumbler of Jack Daniels, he wondered where Gilles was and how he felt.

Chapter Twenty

The humidity washed over him and saturated him when he stepped onto the street from the Port-au-Prince airport. It took time to adjust, and as soon as he got in the taxi, he stuck his head out a window for the breeze. It never really helped all that much, but it was necessary to make the effort anyway. The driver noticed, and Donovan saw him grinning in the rearview mirror.

"Your first time in Port-au-Prince?" the driver said. He had a gold tooth that flashed when he grinned.

"I was here one other time," Donovan said.

"Yes?" the driver said. "Recently?"

Donovan shook his head.

"No. A while ago."

"I see," the driver said. "And now you have come back."

"Now I've come back, yes. "

"You are American?"

"I am, yes."

"I have driven many Americans. Americans are very welcome in Haiti."

"I wondered about that," Donovan said more to himself than the driver.

"It is true—we love Americans here," the driver said, perhaps more strenuously than he really believed, Donovan figured. A good tip hung in the balance.

"How do you feel about Baby Doc leaving?" Donovan said abruptly.

The driver glanced in the mirror. His face was no longer grinning.

"I feel nothing for Baby Doc. He is gone. He must stay gone. I spit on Baby Doc."

The driver spat out his window.

Well, that's clear enough, Donovan thought. But you would not have dared while Baby Doc was still here.

"Are things better?" Donovan said. "Truly?"

"Things are correct again. No more Baby Doc."

The driver spat out the window again.

"How are the people?" Donovan said.

"The people are happy. Very happy."

"That's good."

"Yes, it is very good. Haiti is correct again. All is normal."

"I will drink rum later to Haiti," Donovan said.

"Rhum Barbancourt," the driver said. "I can recommend it."

Donovan smiled thinly.

"I used to know someone who recommended it, the Rhum Barbancourt."

"A wise man, I think," the driver said, nodding.

"Yes, I thought so, too."

* * *

There was a pleasant sidewalk café in front of his hotel that was shaded by palm trees whose fronds rubbed together softly when the breeze came up. Donovan ate red snapper for lunch and then sipped a Prestige beer and watched people walk by. It was a mix of Haitians and Europeans. Americans, too, and he could spot them easily. They were louder than others, their notions of tourist attire often ridiculous.

By his second Prestige, he felt he ought to concoct some sort of plan. Or maybe not. Time would tell. Maybe he would just be a tourist. Maybe he would stay a week. Maybe longer. He had emptied his savings account and could ride a while. Something would come to him. Waiting for it to surface—that was the plan.

His parents – especially his mother – were skeptical when he told them he was leaving again for Haiti. But she had learned he would now make his own choices and that they were indeed his choices to make. She had finally accepted that all that church business was behind him. But he went to Mass with her one time before leaving, and she was ever so pleased.

A blue Peugeot abruptly pulled to the curb, just a few feet from Donovan's table. The driver leaned his head out the window.

It was Gilles.

Donovan took a moment to process his face.

"Shouldn't you be in Paris?" Donovan said.

"I should be, yes. And I was. But now I am here."

"You're back because of Baby Doc?"

Gilles grinned.

"I was told it is an opportunity."

"Sounds familiar."

"As you well know, my friend."

"How did you find me, Gilles?"

"You do remember who I work for, right?"

"How could I forget all those CIA campouts under the stars. Toasting marshmallows and singing hearty songs."

"You have an interesting memory."

"I guess I do. So, you looked for me?"

"I always look for *opportunities*."

"Are there many now in Haiti?"

"It is a new day, Donovan. Much is possible."

"And no more Baby Doc."

"Praise the Lord, as they say in the church."

"I wouldn't know what they say in the church."

"I will note that, my friend."

"So, Gilles, where are you headed in such a shiny new Peugeot?"

"To Les Cayes, my friend."

"I see. Les Cayes. I believe I've heard of it."

"I am sure you have."

"Yes, it's ringing a bell now. They have good rum there, I'm told."

"Rhum Barbancourt," Gilles said. "You were told correctly."

"Besides Rhum Barbancort, what is in Les Cayes these days?"

"Old friends. Comrades. And of course – opportunities. It is a good day for it. But maybe rain later."

Donovan could now clearly visualize Michel, Jean-Paul, and Christophe.

"But the rain never stopped us, Gilles."

"No, it could not."

"If it ever snowed here, that would not have stopped us, either."

"For snow, my friend, you will need to finally hike up

Pic La Selle."

"Maybe I will."

"But I cannot guarantee it actually snows up there."

"Worth the hike regardless."

"Until then, why not come along, Donovan – to Les Cayes."

"Why should I?"

"Because there are old friends of yours there."

"Comrades?"

"In every sense of the word."

Donovan nodded. He didn't know anyone in Port-au-Prince, but that was not the case in Les Cayes. He supposed Gilles was correct—Les Cayes was a place for opportunities. He let out a long sigh, put more than enough bills on the table, and stood, a grin spreading.

"Well, why the hell not, Gilles. I don't have anything better to do."

"Just keep telling yourself that," Gilles said as Donovan slid into the Peugeot next to him.

After they had left Port-au-Prince well behind, Donovan said, "So, just what will we be doing in Les Cayes, if you don't mind me asking? You know—before we actually get there."

"I do not mind at all, my friend. But do you really need to know?"

Donovan looked at the thick, green jungle lining both sides of the road. He was ready for something. Anything. Everything.

"No, not really."

"Then, welcome back, Donovan."

"It's good to *be* back."

About the Author

MICHAEL LOYD GRAY, a member of the Society of Midland Authors, has published six novels and more than forty stories.

He is the winner of the 2005 Alligator Juniper Fiction Prize, 2005 The Writers Place Award for Fiction, and a support grant from the Elizabeth George Foundation.

Gray earned a MFA from Western Michigan University and a bachelor's from the University of Illinois. He lives in Kalamazoo, Michigan, where he collects electric guitars and roots for the Chicago Bears.